WITCH NEMESIS IN WESTERHAM

Paranormal Investigation Bureau Book 16

DIONNE LISTER

Dionne Lister

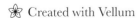

CHAPTER 1

"Lily, what in all the gods' names have you done now?" Will's low, urgent voice and his shoving my arm woke me.

"Huh?" I'd been lying on my back, happily dreaming of eating double-chocolate muffins with my besties, Imani and Liv. Dream cupcakes were almost as good as real ones, and you didn't pay the weight price afterwards. Being woken in the middle of eating one was a total downer. I'd need a real one to make everything better.

I grunted and opened my eyes to our dim room, a strip of morning light peeking from where the blinds met the window. I blinked, not quite trusting my view in the gloom.

Little round eyes, lots of them, stared at me. Those beady eyes were attached to squirrels. Some of them were sitting on my legs, some were in the gap between me and Will, and some were on the other side of me, and a couple were on Will's legs. My mouth dropped open. "What the hell?" I loved squirrels, but waking up to fifteen of them staring at you like creepy stalkers was too much even for me.

"You created this somehow, so you tell me?" Will looked at me and raised a brow.

I shrugged. "It's not like I sent out an invite or anything. How do they even know where our bedroom is?"

That's when I caught movement on my study table. Abby, my adopted cat, sat there, as elegant as you please. She brought her paw up to her mouth and licked it as if everything was normal. She refused to meet my gaze. Will followed my line of sight. "So, it's not your fault."

I rolled my eyes. "Why is everything automatically my fault? Haven't you heard of innocent until proven guilty?"

He looked back at the squirrels, who were still eyeballing us. Did they ever blink? "Yes, but I know you. You're usually at the centre of stuff when it goes south."

One of the squirrels twitched its tail. They wouldn't attack, would they? Nah, they loved me. Surely they weren't here to murder us. When I'd wanted to create a squirrel army, I never envisaged that they could turn on me. "Can you ask Abby what they want?" I still hadn't worked out how to talk to animals. I held out hope that it would happen soon.

"Abby, why are we surrounded by a furry horde?" Will asked. She stopped licking her paw and looked at Will. She meowed a few times. Will grunted and shook his head. He turned to me. "Apparently they've missed you and were worried something had happened. They wanted proof of life." He smirked, and he shook with contained laughter.

I bit my lip, then laughed. "Wow, go away for a week, and have a few days to recover once I'm home, and that's all it takes? I'll have to explain to them whenever we go away." My forehead tightened. "Do they even have a concept of time? It's not like they use calendars or watches."

"They probably don't, and I'm pretty sure they can't count either. It's probably a lost cause."

I cast my gaze over the caring fluffballs and smiled. "You're all so adorable. Thank you for checking on me. I'm fine. Do you guys want some breakfast?" Chittering broke out. One of them scampered around the bed, setting the others off until the bedroom was a crazified zone of cuteness. I laughed. "I guess I'd better get up before someone gets hurt."

I climbed over Will, who grabbed me and gave me a kiss before letting me go on my way. I magicked clothes on and hurried to the bathroom. Once all the morning business was done, I tracked downstairs, a crowd of squirrels behind me. The grey mass followed me out to the backyard, where I magicked nuts and seeds into their bowls. They jumped onto the bench seats, then the table, and sat at their squirrel-size version. Two of them looked at me, and I swear they gave me a nod of thanks. "You're welcome. And thanks for worrying about me."

My mother's laughter came from behind me. "You and those squirrels."

I turned around. "What? They're totally adorable, and they're my friends."

She shook her head. "You're a nut, so I guess you go well with those animals."

It was then I noticed her outfit, and my heart constricted. "What are you up to today?"

Her expression morphed into serious. "Angelica and I have been talking about it for a while, and… well… I'm going back to work for the PIB. I'm going to be Angelica's assistant, help her with field work, reports, that kind of thing."

Without her magic, she'd be almost helpless against any witches who wanted to do her harm, and if she was accompanying Angelica out to catch criminals…. "But you have to be careful. And are you sure you're ready for this? It's bound to bring up things you need to forget."

Mum lifted her chin and folded her arms, her gaze unwavering and stern. "I won't be in danger. I'm not going out to catch criminals, just investigate the crime scenes. I'll leave the capturing to Angelica and the other agents. I think sitting around here all day is worse. I need something to do to keep my mind active. And I need to make a difference. What's the point of having survived if I don't do anything with my life? Not to mention, what else am I qualified for that I'd enjoy?"

I sighed. She had a good point, well, several actually. Knowing she was right did nothing to make me less worried, but who was I to argue? It was her life, and it was her call how she lived it. The fact that her job was what got her taken from James and me in the first place shouldn't come into it. Ah, who the hell was I trying to kid? It did matter, and I wasn't going to like it. At all. But there was nothing I could do, and I didn't want to create friction between us when we were just getting to know each other again.

Guilt nudged me in the ribs because I couldn't bring myself to smile and be joyful for her. The only thing I could manage was a calm "Just be careful."

"I will. Don't worry." She smiled. "It'll be like old times. I'm so excited. I can't wait!" Wow, she was ridiculously enthusiastic about it. "Anyway, I have to go now. Angelica's ready, and I don't want to keep her waiting." She approached me, gave me a hug, then went inside.

I turned back to watch the breakfasting squirrels. If only

everything in life could be as cute and harmless as my grey furballs. But that was impossible. Depressingly impossible, as the morning would soon prove.

CHAPTER 2

Everyone was back at work, so after trying to find some Zen watching the squirrels eat, I wandered up to Costa for some breakfast of my own. The sky was overcast, but it was a balmy twenty-four degrees—T-shirt and shorts weather, even for me. I'd managed to only look over my shoulder four times on the way, which was an improvement on last time, but the edginess I'd had to hold onto during RP times wasn't going away any time soon.

I also made sure I never left home without a return to sender up.

I bought my standard cappuccino and chocolate muffin and found a window seat. After my first sip of coffee, some of the tension left my shoulders. Happy chatter bounced around the café, and there were plenty of smiling people walking past. Seemed as if the warmer weather brought joy along with it. Summer had finally arrived.

I'd just finished my breakfast when my phone rang. Will's

name flashed on the screen. Was he making sure I was okay? "Hello. Miss me already?"

He didn't laugh, which wasn't a good sign. "Would you hate me if I said no?"

"Maybe. It depends why."

"We have a situation, and we need your help. Can you meet me at the bureau ASAP?"

My heartbeat sped up. "Is my mum okay?"

"It's nothing to do with her. A woman's been run over and killed, and we need your help. I don't want to say anything else over the phone. How long until you can get here?"

"I'm just finishing up at Costa. I'll be there in ten. Bye."

"Bye."

As much as I was always happy to help, it would've been nice to have had some more time people watching out the window, observing life go by in my favourite English town. Okay, so I hadn't visited all the places in the UK, but this was pretty, the people were friendly, and I'd made a life here. It really felt like home, and I loved everything about it. And that reminded me that I needed to get out and about more now that I could. There were so many places to visit in the UK, and I was way behind schedule.

I stood and shrugged off the thought. Today I wasn't visiting a park, cathedral, or cute village—I was going to a murder scene. It was time to steel myself and engage PIB mode.

I got home, magicked my PIB uniform on, and made my doorway to headquarters' reception room. It had been a few weeks since I'd been here, a nice few weeks actually. I wasn't really overjoyed to be back, but everyone I loved was here, so I guessed it couldn't be that bad. To be honest, if Chad were gone, the desire to be here would increase exponentially.

I pressed the buzzer, and Gus answered. He grinned. "Miss Lily! Long time no see. How was your holiday?"

I smiled. Good old Gus. He was definitely one part of this place that I always had time for. He was one of the special ones. We hadn't told anyone about Angelica's disappearance or my almost dying, so I gave him the sanitised version of our holiday. "It was fantastic, thank you. Venice is such an interesting place. The food was amazing, the sights were beautiful, and it was great to spend time with everyone away from work. How have you been?"

We walked along the hallway and made it to the lift. I'd expected Will to meet me. Hopefully we weren't going to the conference room and Chad. "I've been well, thank you. We've been minding a lamb for my cousin. He's had to go away for two days, and the lamb needs feeding, so my wife is doing it." The lift arrived, and we got in. Gus pressed the button for the floor above. Argh, looked like we were going to the conference room. I deflated just a little.

"Oh, how adorable!" So far, his story was cute, but my stomach clenched in anticipation for it to turn gross. Even though I'd asked Gus to not talk about anything to do with poo, wee, or vomit, I wasn't sure about his self-control or memory.

He shook his head as the doors opened on the next level. "You'd think, but me missus is keeping him inside, and there's been accidents, if you know what I mean. Also, some dung was stuck under his foot from my cousin's farm, and he stunk the house out. We couldn't figure what it was until it fell out of his hoof. Such a small amount creates such a huge stink." His expression was one of wonder. I was sure my face looked like I wanted to vomit.

"Oh, wow. Um, great." What else could one say to that?

Time to change the subject. "So, what's been happening while we were away?"

"Oh, lots of things." His face grew serious, and he looked behind us before answering. "Not all of them good. Things are going downhill. Your brother is doing his best, but I don't know how long we'll all have jobs for." He lowered his voice to a whisper. "I heard c h a d talking—he forgets I'm there, or he doesn't care because who am I. Anyway, he was talking about cutting numbers further and maybe closing the whole thing down."

I gasped. "Oh my God! What the hell?"

He cringed. "Shh. Keep your voice down."

"Sorry," I whispered. "The shock of it is just, well…." Hmm, how had Angelica managed to bring my mother in as an assistant if they weren't approving new recruits? Was she paying her out of her own pocket? And if everything shut down, what would they all do for jobs? Not to mention what would happen when the witchy criminal element found out they had free rein. "That would be a disaster."

"You're not wrong, Miss Lily." He stopped whispering. "Anyway, we're here." He knocked, then opened the reception-room door.

Blech. Stupid Chad was at the head of the table, his feet resting on its surface, as usual. I flicked my gaze to Will and raised a brow in question. Why hadn't he warned me? Maybe he hadn't known a meeting was going down until after he called? His return expression was one with slightly widened eyes. So, this was a new development, one that wasn't supposed to happen. Of course it was.

Chad gave me the once over and frowned. "Always late. Hurry up."

Well, excuse me. I would've said something, but James,

who was sitting to Chad's right, gave me a subtle head shake. Beren was sitting next to James, and his expression was overly dark, considering it was just a meeting. I knew Chad was a pain in the bum, but Beren usually managed to retain a pleasant demeanour, or at least a poker face.

Imani and Liv had their backs to me. I sat next to Liv. Angelica, my mother, and Millicent were absent, likely working on other cases—lucky them. I folded my arms and glared at Chad. "Well, I'm here now. What's up?" Will's jaw flexed. I knew I shouldn't poke the bear, but he started it, and, to be honest, the words were out before I thought to clamp my lips shut.

Chad narrowed his eyes at me, then turned to James. "Explain to your belligerent sister what's going on." Wow, that was a big word for Chad to use. I hadn't thought him capable. Maybe he'd been reading the dictionary in his spare time.

James took a breath. "A… woman called Alison Carter, a witch, was run over in the early hours of this morning while walking home from work. She was found at the side of the road. Her injuries are consistent with being hit by a car, and there was no magic signature found on her body."

Call me stupid, but I didn't see why I was here. "So, she could've been killed by a non-witch? Was there any paint or tyre tracks from the car?"

"No, but we'd like to visit the scene of the crime again and get your take on it." By that, he meant my photos, but why the hell was he asking me in front of Chad? He didn't know my secret, and because of his stupidity and propensity to feel threatened by those better than him, he was the last person I wanted to know it.

"But why me? I mean, I know I've helped in the past,

but…." I shrugged. James wouldn't say anything about my talent here, but I wanted to know what they'd told Chad.

Chad turned to me and gave a punchy nod. "That's exactly what I said. You're nobody. You're not even a trained agent. Apparently, your brother thinks you might notice something they haven't because of your keen eye for detail, since you're a photographer."

"You never know. I'm happy to help, of course, but I'm not sure if I can." I played it cool.

"Good." James looked at Imani. "If you could interview Miss Carter's colleagues, that would be a good start."

"Can do. I'll get started straight away." She stood, then made her doorway in the space between the table and the door. She stepped through.

James turned his gaze on Liv. "I'd like you to search through her social media for any clues on who else, other than her work mates and family, we need to interview. I'm assuming this was an accident, but we need to rule out foul play."

"I'll get on that straight away."

"Thanks."

Beren turned to James. "What about me?"

Liv gave him a concerned look across the table. There was something going on here that I didn't know about. What had I missed?

James's tone was gentle. "For now, nothing. I let you sit in on this so you would know what we were doing. I think it's best if you help Millicent with her case today. You're too close to this."

Beren snorted out a frustrated breath. "Dammit. Let me help."

"There's nothing you can do that we can't."

"What about if I interview her family? They know me.

Surely they'll tell me more than they'd tell any of the other agents."

"I don't know." James drummed his fingers on the table. "What if there are things they don't want to tell you because they don't want to hurt your feelings… like maybe she was seeing someone?"

Beren shook his head. "That won't hurt me anymore." He gazed across the table at Liv. "The woman I love is sitting right there. It's shocking, and, yes, I'm upset about what's happened, but not so upset that I can't do my job properly." And the plot thickened. Ex-girlfriend, maybe? I'd have to wait to find out. There was no way I was going to ask right now.

James looked to Will, and Chad's top lip rose in a sneer. I'd bet my favourite squirrel that he was put out because James wasn't deferring to him. Ha ha, bad luck. I didn't bother hiding my smile.

Whatever Will conveyed was so subtle that I missed it, but James nodded. "Okay, you interview her parents and two brothers."

"Thank you. I appreciate it."

James turned to Chad. "That's all I need."

Chad's feet slammed on the ground as his chair flew backwards. He couldn't do anything with subtlety. He stood and planted his hands on his hips. "Don't screw this up." He made a doorway and left. What a weirdo.

Will stood and looked at me. "We're driving."

"Okay, cool."

We all headed for the door, while Liv hugged Beren and whispered something to him. He nodded and buried his face in her neck. Now I really wanted to know his history with the dead woman.

I waited until we were in the basement and walking to

Will's black Range Rover to ask. "So, what's the deal with B and the dead woman?"

"They dated for a year." Will unlocked the car, and we got in. I let James sit in the front because he was working. I was tagging along.

"How long ago?"

Will started the car. "They broke up about six months before you arrived. He was in love. She broke it off with him. He didn't take it well at first, but he got over her eventually. He'd been planning on asking her to marry him."

My mouth dropped open. "Wow, it was serious, at least for him. That's sad. But now he's got Liv, and she's alive, so it all worked out for the best."

James turned and scowled at me. "Lily! You sure come out with some horrible stuff sometimes. Seriously."

"What? I'm just looking at the bright side. As if you're not thinking it."

"I wasn't, no."

I rolled my eyes. Big brothers could be so annoying. "What do you need from me? Am I taking a picture of the car?"

James turned back to look out the windscreen. "Yes, thank you."

"Are we doing a super special investigation because it's someone Beren knew?"

James and Will briefly looked at each other. Will, "Even though we're making out like it was an accident—for Beren's sake—she was run over on the footpath and sent flying into the road. Unless someone lost control of their car at just the wrong moment, it was deliberate."

"Oh my God. That's horrific." Heaviness settled in my stomach. "Do you think it was someone she knew or someone who was out to kill a random person?"

James said, "We don't know at this stage. We're hoping you can help us with that."

"Okay."

We were quiet for the rest of the car ride. Twenty-five minutes later, Will pulled into the parking lot of the Stag and Hunter pub. It sat on the corner of the main road and another street. I checked my return to sender was up, and we got out. I followed James and Will about fifty metres along the side street, which seemed to be fairly quiet. Cars were parked on one side, but it was too narrow for parking on the other. A few shops lined the road, then houses. "And no one saw anything?" I asked. "You said the early hours of the morning, but don't pubs close by about eleven or twelve?"

Will nodded. "Yes. This one shut at eleven thirty, but there's nothing to say the bar staff can't hang around for drinks afterwards. We're not sure of the exact time of death, but the initial assumption based on the body is between two and four in the morning." He stopped walking where the blue-and-white tape started. "This is where it happened."

The path on the side of the street where no cars were parked was about two metres from the street, with people's fences bordering the other side of it. "They wouldn't have had to veer far in order to hit here. Maybe a drunk driver or someone on their phone?"

James turned to me. "Why don't we stop guessing and see if you can clear it up?"

"Ooh, testy. You could ask nicely."

His jaw muscles bunched. "I have no patience today, Lily. Save it."

"What's got your knickers in a knot?" I wracked my brain and finally came up with something. "Is it Mum going back to work?"

Surprise registered in his eyes for a split second before he shut it down. "Yes. Now's not the time to talk about it. Can we just get this happening?"

"Okay." I pulled my phone out of my pocket and drew on my magic. I wasn't looking forward to seeing someone die, yet again, and I took a deep breath. "Show me the car that hit and killed Alison Carter."

Day turned to night. Street lights wanly illuminated sections of the street and footpath. A car appeared where we were standing, coming from the direction of the pub. I shivered and moved out of the way.

"Lily!" Will shouted and grabbed my arm, pulling me to him.

I blinked and looked at the car that just drove where I'd been going to walk. Crap. My heart hammered, and my breathing quickened. "Oh my God. Thank you."

"Jesus, Lily. You should know better than that." James gave me his best your-big-brother-is-disappointed-in-you look.

"I know. I'm sorry. It's not like I want to die. Sometimes, I just get so caught up in what I'm doing that I forget. When I look at those pictures, it's like I'm there."

Will's grip tightened on my arm for a moment; then he let go. "Please pay attention."

"Okay." I stood outside the taped area but in front of the car and Alison. She was walking towards me, the car behind her moving in the same direction. I asked my question again, and the scene sprang to life in front of me. I quickly changed it to video mode. It didn't happen often, so when it did, it always took me off guard.

It was hard to hold my position when everything was moving towards me. I glanced around, then took a few steps backwards. Alison hadn't stood a chance. At first, she was oblivious, probably because she thought whatever car she'd heard would drive past, but when the sound was directly behind her, she jerked around in time to see her fate but not escape it. The car ploughed into her, and her body rolled up onto the bonnet, hit the windscreen, then flew into the air and landed on the road behind the car. I spun quickly and videoed the car getting away, until the vision stopped, and daylight showed in my screen once more.

My hand shook slightly as I handed the phone to James. Will watched the video with him, their faces grim. Will's forehead wrinkled. "It's too dark to see the driver or get a proper colour on the car, but it's a dark car—maybe black, red, dark green, or navy blue. At least we know it's an older BMW, and we have the number plate."

They replayed it two more times, and James handed my phone back and pulled his out. He called Liv. "Hey, Liv. Can you run this plate for me?" He gave her the number. "Thanks." James killed the call and looked at me. "Thanks, Lily. That's going to blow our case wide open. We'll just have to figure out a way to find the car without revealing your involvement." He looked around the street, at the buildings. "Maybe someone has security video at one of the houses along here. It's a long shot that any of it will be at the right angle to show the number plate, but we can try."

"Why didn't you just do that in the first place?" I asked.

James shrugged. "It's time-consuming to get warrants and then canvas every house in the street. Why do it if we know there was nothing to get. Maybe the guy had taken his number plates off? At least we know there is something to find, so the time will be worth every minute."

"Fair enough. So, is that all you need from me?"

James nodded. "For now. Depending on what our interviews turn up, we might need you later." We headed back to the car, but James didn't get in. "I'll go help Imani with the interviews and catch a ride with her. I'll see you two later."

Five minutes down the road, Will's phone rang. He answered it with the car's Bluetooth. "Hey, Liv. What've you got for me?" That was weird. Why hadn't she called James?

"Um… hi. You're not going to like this." Her voice was shaky.

"What's wrong, Liv?"

"Hi, Lily. Pretty much everything right now."

My shoulders tensed. "What are you talking about?"

"I found who that car is registered to."

When she didn't keep going, Will said, "And?"

"Beren."

"What?!" I sat up straight in my seat, my eyes wide. That didn't make sense.

"Did you check your garage before you left this morning?" asked Will.

"No. We never do, but it wasn't one of those cars. It was the classic BMW he's got in the storage place."

Will put his blinker on and turned left. "The Sunday car?"

"Yes, but we haven't been in it for a couple of months. I haven't told him yet because he's still at Alison's parents' place. Plus, I don't want him freaking out. Do you think you could go and check it out without making a fuss?"

"You mean without telling anyone else?" Will's eyebrow rose.

"Yes. I'm sorry to ask, but I have no idea what Chad will do when he finds out. You know he's looking for any excuse to get rid of us, and he'd lock Beren up in an instant."

"Was he home with you all night?" Hopefully she wouldn't be offended by my question.

"Of course he was."

"Well, you have nothing to worry about, then." I looked at Will.

He glanced at me, then back at the road. "We'll head over there now. I'll let you know what we find out."

"Thanks, Will. I owe you one." She hung up.

Will chucked a U-turn and sped down the road. His expression oscillated between angry and confused. I didn't want to ask, but sitting here in silence was like waiting for a bomb to go off. I couldn't stand it anymore. "What are you thinking?"

"Beren's been framed. There's no way he would ever hit someone with a car and keep on driving. And he would never intentionally kill someone unless it was in the line of duty and he had no other choice."

"Who would do this to him? I mean, other than people he's helped put in jail, he wouldn't have any enemies. He's, like, the nicest person I know."

"I know. I have no idea." He glanced at me for a second. "I just hope your photos tell us what we want to know."

"Surely there'd be security footage at the storage place."

"True, but we'd need a warrant."

"Which you'd easily get if you asked."

"But how did we trace it this far? We supposedly don't have the registration number of that car."

"Oh, yeah." I sighed. Having to keep my talent a secret was super annoying. Except, knowing stupid Chad, he'd probably think I was lying and doctoring the photos somehow. Not that Chad would be dumb enough to say I'd framed my own friend…. Although, one should never assume.

The closer we got to the warehouse, the more severe the nausea became. Bubbling in my stomach, it was pushing towards my throat, and I had to keep swallowing. I just couldn't believe Beren would do anything like that. He'd never even mentioned her in the whole time I'd known him, and he and Liv were so happy. Which was why I knew he didn't do it. We just had to prove who did.

Hopefully we'd solve it all before anyone else became aware of our information. With a bit of luck, that car would be back at the storage facility, not sitting on a street somewhere waiting for the police to find it.

It started raining, which was a perfect accompaniment to our journey. I folded my arms and stared out the window. Why we couldn't go a few weeks without drama, I had no idea, and my day had started off so well—squirrels in bed, then a delicious chocolate muffin for breakfast. Maybe things would calm down again before bedtime?

If I believed that, I'd believe anything.

CHAPTER 3

The storage unit was in Royal Tunbridge Wells, almost twenty miles south of Westerham. When we got to the security gate of a modern factory complex, Will had to show ID to get admittance. He had to sign his name and the time he entered as well. Security cameras watched from left and right—there was no getting in or out of here without being noticed, unless you used magic.

Will found storage unit eighteen and parked in front of it. The blue-grey roller door was shut. Will's magic tickled my scalp, and we heard a click. Then the door opened automatically.

The large single garage was empty.

Bummer.

Will gave me a nod; then he wandered around the space. What he was looking for, I had no idea—maybe a magic signature or something? I pulled out my phone, hoping to be able to prove Beren's innocence, even if it was just for Liv, Will, and me to know. I stood at the border between the inside of the unit and outside. I was assuming the car had been facing towards the door when it was parked. I drew my magic. "Show me who drove the car last time it left this garage."

The light dimmed. An overhead strip light did a barely adequate job of illuminating the interior of the garage. But it showed me what I needed to know.

I wished it hadn't.

A man had just opened the door of the forest-green BMW. His left leg was already in the footwell. I clicked a shot and took a shuddering breath. I walked closer and zoomed in. *Click.*

There was no mistaking who it was.

I lowered my camera and stared at the now-empty space. But it wasn't possible.

"Lily? Lily?"

I blinked. "Oh, um, sorry." I didn't have the heart to say anything, so I just handed Will my camera. My voice had lost its will to be heard and came out at little more than a whisper. "There has to be an explanation. There just has to be."

As soon as he saw the photo, his eyebrows rose, and he zoomed in on the image. He stared and stared until he didn't look like he was actually looking at the photo. His thoughts had gone somewhere else. He shook his head, then met my gaze and handed me the camera. "There has to be another explanation."

"I know." Because if there wasn't…. "So, how are we going to do this? We can't actually prove anything without my camera unless we access security video, which we can't do un—"

"I know. We should talk to Beren, but that's against the rules." The evidence we'd found clearly implicated Beren, and since he was a friend and colleague, Will shouldn't be the one

WITCH NEMESIS IN WESTERHAM

to question him or give him a heads up. The fact that we were going to keep this information secret from Chad and follow it up ourselves was a total conflict of interest.

"But Liv knows about the car."

"I think we're all going to have to wait until the car is found and linked to the crime and hope that Liv doesn't say anything to Beren. The fact that the crime happened on that street is enough to get a warrant for any security videos." He sighed, and he scratched his head. "I'm going to have to tell James, but I don't want to do it on the phone. Come on. Let's go to Angelica's. I'll text him to meet us there when he's done with the interviews."

I rubbed Will's back. What a craptastic situation to be in. "But what about Liv's alibi for him?"

He sighed. "She could've lied, or he could have put a sleep spell on her and gone out. He could have mind wiped her, and she wouldn't know. He could've done any number of things."

My forehead tightened. "But this is Beren we're talking about. Do you really believe he'd do any of that or kill his ex?" Not to mention that Liv wasn't a lying kind of person. But how far would she go to protect the man she loved? I thought back to when her ex-fiancé had embezzled and cheated. She'd been shocked, but she hadn't refused to believe anything when shown what he'd done. No, I couldn't believe she'd lied.

Will's Adam's apple bobbed as he swallowed. "No, but it's hard to ignore the evidence on your phone." His eyes shut for a moment. When they opened, the angst had disappeared, hidden behind his impeccable poker face. "Come on. We need to let Angelica know."

The evidence was there, but I couldn't believe it, and I was pretty sure Will was struggling with that, too, but he had to do his job. We just had to cling to the fact that there was another explanation, and it wasn't what it looked like, because the alternative was too much to bear.

After a tense forty-five-minute wait for James, he and Imani showed up in her car. The four of us sat in the living room—Will next to me on one Chesterfield, and Imani and James sat on the one opposite. Abby wove around Will's legs before jumping up to sit in his lap. She was a good cat who knew when someone needed her. Will stroked her back as he spoke. "Liv got back to me about the number plate."

James furrowed his brow. "Why didn't she call me?"

"Because the car belongs to Beren." Will stared at my brother, whose mouth had dropped open. Imani looked at me as if to say, no way; tell me this is a joke.

I shook my head. "It's not a joke. Here. These are the photos I took at the storage place where he keeps the car. When we went today, it wasn't there." I handed my phone to James, and he and Imani looked at the two pictures I'd taken.

James shut his eyes for a minute, probably trying to figure out how it couldn't be true. He opened them again. "This is so hard to believe. Beren, of all people. He would never run someone down on purpose. He's not a psycho."

"It doesn't make sense." Imani took the phone from James, peered closely at the photo, then handed the phone back to me.

It totally didn't make sense. "Liv said he was home all night, and I believe her. Is there a spell where you can make yourself look like someone else? Or could someone have stolen it from wherever Beren parked it last?"

Will looked at me. "A spell to look like someone else? No…

well, nothing that would work on witches. You could possibly do it to fool non-witches, but it's like a no-notice spell. You'd also need to be an expert and very powerful to make an illusion like that stick. I don't even think it would fool a video camera. As for parking it somewhere else, Liv said they hadn't driven it for two months. We'll have to confirm with Beren whether he left it in storage."

"Maybe there's a guy who hates Beren, and he had an operation to look like him so he could frame him for this and ruin his life?" Yes, I was scraping the bottom of the barrel, but my brain wouldn't accept that he could've done this.

Imani cocked her head to the side. "I'm afraid that's a bit far-fetched, love. None of us want to believe it, but we need a plausible answer."

"We need to talk to Beren, see what he has to say." James was ever the sensible one, and he had a talent that could tell when someone was lying. "It's probably better if it's just Will and I who speak to him."

"You won't get any argument from me, love."

"Imani's right," I said. "What are you going to do if he's guilty?"

James looked at me, sorrow and regret radiating from his eyes. "Arrest him."

My stomach dropped. I had no words. I wanted to warn Liv, but that was probably against protocol, and what would it achieve? "What do I do if Liv rings me?" Which was a possibility since she knew we'd checked out the storage.

Will and James looked at each other; then Will said, "I'll give her a call, tell her we're going to talk to Beren and get back to her afterwards. I don't want to do it at headquarters though."

James rubbed his forehead. "We have to do it at headquarters. If he is guilty and we let him get away, that's going to be enough to get us suspended, plus a full enquiry, and then they're going to ask how we got to that conclusion, and unless you want to give Lily's secret away, I don't see how we can explain ourselves."

Imani pursed her lips. "You know, even if you interview him and arrest him, God forbid, we'll still need proof. You'll have to wait and get those security tapes from the crime scene… if there are any. We can't do anything until you have them."

James smacked himself in the forehead. "Thank God someone's on the ball here."

"Don't beat yourself up, love. This has come as a shock to all of us, and you and Will are his best mates. You're bound to not be thinking straight."

"So now what?" I asked. "Shouldn't we also be looking at who has it in for him? I know what my photos show, but I also know what my heart says. We know him, and none of us can believe he'd do this. Surely that has to count for something?"

Will sighed. "We get the warrants for that evidence, and we go through whatever security footage we need to until we have our proof, then we question B. At this stage, Lily, that's all we can do. Once we've done that, we can possibly look into who would want to see Beren go to jail." His "once we've done that" meant that if Beren denied it. Of course he would. Wouldn't he?

Imani stood. "Right. Let's get to this. Hopefully B will have a good explanation once we question him." She looked at me. "In the meantime, just tell Liv you didn't find anything."

My eyes widened. "I can't lie to her."

"I'm afraid Imani's right, Lily. There's no telling what she'll do if she finds out we've confirmed that he was the last one to drive it away from the storage facility, and we don't want her tipping him off about the photos you've taken—it's evidence against him."

I sucked in a deep breath. I didn't make it a habit of lying to friends unless it was life or death. Lying to Liv went against everything I'd ever done, and this wasn't a small lie. And it wasn't a lie to help her, like a white lie where you told someone a mistake they'd made wasn't as bad as they'd thought, or that those Crocs they loved so much looked fabulous.

James looked at me. "It's for the best, Lily. We wouldn't ask you to do this if it wasn't important."

"I know. It doesn't make it any easier, though." I leaned across and patted Abby. This was going to be the toughest wait ever. By the time they got the warrants and served them to everyone and went through the footage, assuming everyone was home in the next twenty-four hours, it could take two days to get what we needed. "What if no one has camera footage?"

James's phone rang. "Hello, Agent Bianchi speaking." He listened for a while and nodded a couple of times, his face going into poker mode. "Yes. I understand. We'll be there in half an hour." He hung up, and his poker face melted away. I didn't think he could look any more devastated if he'd tried. "That was one of our connections in the local police. They've found the car, which has a smashed windscreen and other damage consistent with hitting someone, and traced it back to Beren."

I covered my mouth with my hand. God no. This was escalating quickly. Beren might be in jail by the end of the day. Although, they had to prove someone else didn't steal it, and that would involve getting security footage from where he'd stored the car. Still, if that footage was as incriminating as my photos…. I blinked back tears. And what was Liv going to think? Crap.

Will ran a hand through his hair, then gripped his scalp. He dropped his hand to his lap and addressed James. "I'll call him, ask him to meet us at headquarters." He turned his gaze to Imani. "If one of our group can handle this as much as possible, it would be ideal. It might still be seen as a conflict of interest, but let's ignore that until Chad intervenes. Can you get over to that car now and take Lily with you? Maybe she can take some photos that will give us additional clues. There has to be more to this than what we're seeing." He shook his head.

James's face was grim. "I hate to say it, but as the evidence piles up, there's only so long we can suspend disbelief. I just hope you're right, and there's something we're not seeing." He stood and sighed. "Let's get this over with. I'll meet you at headquarters." He moved to the middle of the room, made his doorway, and left.

What a disaster.

Will pulled out his phone and called Beren. "Hey. How's the interview going?" He listened for a while and made noncommittal "I'm listening" noises. "Okay. Can you meet me at headquarters? James's office ASAP. It's about this case. We've found some new evidence. Okay. Bye." Will placed Abby on my lap, stood, and put his phone in his pocket. "He's just finishing up with Alison's parents now. They're witches, so he travelled there. He'll be back at headquarters in a few minutes." Will's chest rose as he took in a huge breath. He huffed it out and looked at the ceiling, maybe searching for answers that weren't there. He looked down at me. "This is going to suck."

My lips turned down in defeat. "I know. I'm sorry." I

placed Abby on the couch and stood so I could give Will a big hug. It was all I had to offer, which was pathetic, really. "If you need anything, let me know."

He squeezed me back, then dropped his arms. "I will." He moved to the middle of the room, then left.

Imani and I stared at each other. She allowed her sadness and disbelief to show in her face, and I was pretty sure I looked as despondent as she did. But we didn't say anything— what was there to say?

Her phone dinged, breaking our depressing, non-verbal discussion. She looked at the message, then back up at me. "It's the address for Beren's car. We're going to have to drive. It'll be quicker from here than headquarters, and I have my car."

"Cool. Let's get going." I magicked my Nikon to myself because it would look more official to any police or agents on-site.

During the drive, my phone rang. I pulled it out of my pocket. Crap. It was Liv. My heart pounded. How was I supposed to avoid telling her what I'd found? I let it ring out and go to voicemail. I was such a bad friend.

"Who was that?"

"Who do you think?"

Imani glanced at me. "You should've answered it. You can't leave her waiting forever, and now that the car's been found, she might want to talk to you about that."

"But how can I tell her what we found, and on the phone? She's going to ask me for sure. That's not news you just want to blurt out. Surely I should be within hugging distance when I tell her."

"I bet she's more worried now than she would be if you

just told her, but I agree—this news is better imparted in person."

My phone rang again. I blew out a breath and answered it. "Hey, Liv."

"Hey, Lily. I've just heard that they found Beren's car."

"Does he know?"

"Yes. He's in talking with James and Will now, but I have no idea what's going on. What did you guys find at the garage?"

"I can't tell you over the phone. Imani and I are on our way to the car now. As soon as we get back, I'll come see you. Okay?" Silence. "Liv, hello?"

"Yeah, okay. Can you at least tell me if it's good news or bad?"

It was my turn to pause. Crap. "I'm so sorry, Liv."

"Are you sure?"

"Someone could've tampered with things somehow, but at this stage, I can't see how, so I'm as sure as I can be. But I'll fill you in when I get there. Okay?"

Her voice wavered. "Okay. Thanks."

"Hang in there. There has to be a logical answer, and I promise we'll find it. Just sit tight. I'll see you soon."

She sniffled. "Okay, Lily. Bye."

"How did she sound?"

"Not happy, but not panicking. She's pretty tough, but I'm sure she's confused and scared for Beren. Out of everyone I know, he's the least likely person to do something like that."

"I agree. But sometimes we think we know someone, and we find out that we were wrong. I love B, and I'm still not buying that he did it, but I've been down this road before." She put her blinker on, and we turned right into the parking area of a garden centre—Beatrice's Blooms. Whatever her story was, it wasn't the time to ask. A group of two police and two agents surrounded the BMW, which was parked askew across two spaces. "It sure seems like someone wanted to get noticed, or maybe they were in a hurry." Imani parked and killed the engine. She looked at me. "Ready?"

"As I'll ever be." I opened the door and took a deep breath. If I saw Beren through the lens again, it was going to kill me. They really didn't pay me enough to "consult." I wasn't sure if any amount would make me feel better. Probably not. And to be honest, I'd do it for free if it was going to help my friends. I didn't see who I was actually helping this time though… but whatever.

As we reached the law-enforcement group, one of the agents—a tall male, about six foot four—greeted Imani. "Agent Jawara. Long time no see."

"Hi, Agent Smith. It has been a while. Great to see you again. What've you got for me?" I was happy to have no introduction. I just wanted to take my photos without any notice or fanfare.

Agent Smith nodded towards the car. "We think this was the car used in the hit-and-run on Alison Carter." He glanced at the two officers—a young female and a middle-aged male. "We've traced the registration to a Beren DuPree." His eyes gave Imani a meaningful look. At least he wasn't giving away that it was one of the PIB agents. It was nice that they stuck together when things went south. But I couldn't forget that they still had a job to do, and if that job entailed arresting one of their own and shoving them in jail, they'd do it in a heartbeat.

"Okay, thanks." She looked at the two police officers and gave them a smile. "Thanks for attending and getting us word so quickly. My team and I can take it from here."

The male constable gave a nod. "If you need anything, let us know." He turned to his partner and jerked his head towards their police car. They turned and set off. Now the real conversation could begin.

Imani made a bubble of silence. "Have you found any magic signatures?"

Agent Smith shook his head. "No. We'll have it taken to headquarters once you're done. Then we'll search for prints, blood, hair, etcetera." Despite the bubble of silence, he lowered his voice. "Does he know?"

"Yes. They're interviewing him now."

The other agent, a tall, lanky, brown-skinned man with straight hair and a kind face, said, "He's the last agent I'd expect to do this. Agent Bianchi feels the same, and Smith and I'll be going through a list of witches he's recently arrested, see if we can't find something that will explain this."

Imani gave him a strained smile. "Thanks. It certainly is hard to believe he did this, but so far, the evidence isn't looking promising—Agent DuPree never reported the car stolen. But, we all know the kind of person he is, so we're going to give this all we've got. We make a lot of enemies—it's the nature of the job. Anyway, good luck on your search. When are the team turning up to haul this away?"

Smith glanced at the car before looking back at Imani. "Half an hour." His gaze flicked to me for a moment. "You've got time to take your photos, but we'll leave you to keep the site secure until they've taken it away."

Imani tipped her chin up. "That's fine. You've got enough to do. Good luck."

Both agents bade us goodbye and got into a black Porsche. Not very subtle, and with the way they were dressed, they could be drug lords for all anyone knew. I would've chuckled, but this whole situation was way too depressing. And now I had to take more photos. I frowned. Imani looked at me but didn't say anything.

I took the lens cap off and slid it into my pocket, then turned the camera on and held it to my face. "Show me the person who ran over Alison Carter getting out of this car for the last time."

Darkness settled over the parking lot. Two very tall street lights sat at either end of the parking lot, their illumination not striking, but enough to reveal the man getting out of the driver's-side door. A spike of nausea and dizziness struck me. I slammed my hand on my stomach and shut my eyes.

"Lily, are you all right?" Imani's voice came from right next to me.

"Yes," I choked out. *Get it together.* I heaved in a deep breath and opened my eyes. Not wanting to look at Imani for fear of losing my nerve, I asked the question again in my mind. The scene reappeared, and I clicked off three shots—one directly in front of Beren, taking in him and the car, one from the side, and one from behind. Then I stepped close for a head shot from the front and side. I stared through the lens, trying to decipher the look in his eyes. This was a Beren I didn't know… a Beren whose cold expression held a hint of satisfaction.

I lowered my Nikon. It was too much.

Imani gently pried the camera from my hand and went through the photos. She handed my camera back, her expression bleak.

We waited in silence until the tow truck came and took Beren's car away.

Our hope went with it.

CHAPTER 4

On our drive back, James texted Imani, asking us to come straight to his office when we returned. Imani opened the outer door, and we entered James's reception area to shouting coming from the office. Chad. We froze and listened. "I want him arrested!"

James's tone was on the edge of control, his frustration barely contained, like an overblown balloon ready to pop. "My talent, as I've explained, is for truth telling. Everything Agent DuPree said to me in there was honest."

Chad's voice lowered from shouting to just loud and obnoxious. "You don't think your feelings for the man have clouded your interpretation?"

"Not at all." I could just imagine James standing there with his arms folded, giving Chad a cool "I don't make mistakes" look.

"I don't agree. You Brits stick together. You always have, ever since I got here. No one respects me, but you'll learn to by the time I'm done." Silence. Imani and I stared at each other.

What the hell was happening? There was no magic. Chad's voice, quieter this time. "Agent Price, yes. I've had enough of this ridiculousness. Arrest Agent DuPree. Charge him with murder and fleeing the scene of an accident. I want him in a cell within the next fifteen minutes."

My stomach dropped. My magic said Beren was guilty, but my brother's talent said he wasn't. Whatever the truth, there wasn't enough evidence for us to jump one way or the other, and now that Chad had intervened, we had no choice. We couldn't avoid what was happening, and anger still skittered through my body that he'd called in reinforcements. Bloody Chad.

"As of now, Agent Bianchi, you are off this case. I don't trust you or your little group of friends. Agents Blakesley, Jawara, and your wife are banned from this case. I'll assign you something else this afternoon."

James stayed silent. Chad's magic prickled my scalp. The stillness dragged on, the seconds ticking away. He must've made a doorway and left. Good riddance to bad rubbish.

Imani was the first to move. I followed her into my brother's office.

James was at his desk, elbows on the table, head resting in his hands. We all loved Beren, but James was one of his best friends. This must be impossible for him. "Hey," I said as Imani slid out a seat on our side of James's table and sat. I did the same, and James looked up. He didn't bother to mask his feelings—pain emanated from his eyes.

"This has all gone to hell. Show me what you got." He looked at me. Reluctance stayed my hand—it was like sticking the knife in for him to see the images on my camera—but what was the point now? This train ride to the underworld had gathered speed, and I was pretty sure there were no brakes.

The ending was inevitable. All we could do was live through the pain as best we could.

I slid my Nikon across the table.

After looking through the photos, his face twisting in disbelief, he handed my camera back. His magic prickled my scalp, and a glass of water appeared on the table in front of him. He stood, picked it up, and turned. His arm reached back and flew forward, flinging the glass against the wall. It smashed, and water sprayed across the paint, glass and liquid covering the carpet.

I cringed. James was never violent, at least not unless he was trying to take down a criminal. Sudden outbursts weren't his style. I stood and went around the table to give him a hug. Thankfully, he accepted it.

"Right, love. We all think this can't be what it seems, but what if it is?" As much as I hated it, Imani was being sensible right now. We had to consider the two options: innocent or guilty. One was a belief supported by James's talent; the other was backed by harder evidence we couldn't ignore.

James pulled away from me. "Thanks, Lily. Why don't you sit down? We need to nut this out." I moved back to my seat, and James sat, then grabbed his phone off the desk. He called someone. "Will. Yes. My office. Now. Bye."

We all shuffled through our own thoughts until Will arrived. None of us were in the mood to talk about how guilty Beren looked. How had we all gotten him so wrong? Surely if he were capable of mowing an ex-lover down with his car, he wasn't the great guy we'd believed. But none of us were naïve, and my brother's talent was an insurance policy against befriending the wrong people. Will and Imani were seasoned agents, trained to pick out a liar from a hundred paces. Where had we all gone wrong?

But what if we hadn't? Who was going to figure it out and save him from a life in prison? Gah, was I deluding myself? I sighed. Thankfully Will walked in because I didn't know how much longer I could have those useless thoughts circling my brain and not go nuts. Even more depressingly, nuts made me think of squirrels, but in this instance, I couldn't even smile. I sighed again.

Will magicked a chair next to mine and sat. He grabbed my camera and looked through the photos, then set the Nikon aside. He pinned his gaze on James. "We all know what it looks like. So, what now?" Will made a bubble of silence.

James twirled his tie around two fingers as he spoke. "Before we get started, Chad has banned all of us from investigating further. Whatever we do, it's under the radar." We all nodded. That was simple enough to do. It wasn't as if Chad was a genius. We just had to be careful of any brown-nosers who might take it upon themselves to notify Mr Incompetent.

"That was always a risk. I hate to say it, but it was the right call. Even if we find evidence to clear him, it will have to come via another source. Chad isn't going to trust anything we do, based on principal."

I nodded. "Those agents today seemed like they liked Beren. They were just as disbelieving as us."

Imani looked at me, then James. "Lily's right. Agent Smith and Agent Singh. They both quietly offered their support. We can move information through them."

James's fingers stopped drumming. "Agent Singh went through training with us. He's definitely someone we can trust. Smith, I don't know so well, but since he's Singh's partner, it's probably a go." He sat back in his chair and folded his arms. "When I asked Beren if he'd done it, he said no. I know he was telling the truth." He nodded towards my camera. "But that says he wasn't. So, whose talent should we believe?"

Will and Imani looked back and forth between James and me. I put my hands in the air. "I hope we can believe yours. This is one time I don't want to be right." It did raise an interesting point though. Was Chad right about my brother's perspective being skewed by his feelings for Beren? Since Beren was already in jail and believing that took us in no new directions, I was only too happy to consider the other option. "Let's suppose you're right and I'm wrong. Why and how is it possible? What are we missing?"

Imani looked at me. "Has your magic been reliable lately? Have you had any glitches?"

I shook my head and frowned. "Nope. My talent isn't subjective either. I ask a direct question, and I get an answer."

"Mine isn't either, Lily. I just know, and I've never been wrong."

Well, that achieved nothing.

Will leaned forward and looked at James. "Maybe the murderer has figured out a way to spell themselves that fools even witches and scrying talents?"

I scratched my arm. "Is it possible that whoever did this hates Beren so much that he went and had plastic surgery to look like him?"

Imani's brows drew down. "That's highly improbable. And the likeness is incredible. You'd need the best surgeon in the world to get that right."

"Or a witch one. Magic makes things possible that are unbelievable. Surely you can't rule that out?" I wasn't giving up on this line of questioning. It was plausible.

James cocked his head to the side. "But if you hated someone that much, would you want to look like them forever?

There's a lot of pain that goes with that kind of reconstruction. Even if the doctor did a good job and healed the patient, it would still be excruciating for a few days. No witch has that much power to make recovering easier after expending the energy it would take to get that surgery spot on. There's no difference between how Beren looks and the man in the photos." For someone who was hoping he was right, he wasn't making a good case at this point.

Will shrugged. "You know there are lots of crazy people out there. Non-witches don't have the market all sewn up in lunatics. We need to be thinking extreme. And I think that's a good hypothesis."

Still…. "Okay, let's say we believe this for a minute. Who would do this, and why would they hate Beren so much? It can't be someone he put in jail for a long time, or they'd still be in jail. It's not like you'd do that for anyone else just because they asked. And I really think if he helped put someone away for a couple of years, it wouldn't escalate to this."

Imani shook her head. "A child of someone put in jail might do it, a parent, or a lover. Depends how invested they were. Or maybe if you were paid enough."

I raised my brows. "You'd have to be talking a lot of money. I mean, why would you want to look like someone else forever? Plus everyone you know is going to be asking why and maybe not liking it. They've pretty much lost who they are." There was no way I'd do that for anything or anyone. I wasn't exactly a supermodel, but my face was mine, and I knew it and liked it well enough. You could also tell I was related to James and my mum. It'd be weird and awful if I looked like someone else. I was keeping my face, thank you very much. "Honestly, I don't know if this hypothesis stacks up."

Will looked around at us. "Does anyone have any other

ideas? So far, we have two—a never-before-heard-of spell and surgery."

My suggestion was going to be just as likely as the other two, but I figured we had nothing to lose. "There's only one other thing I can think of. Everyone supposedly has a doppelgänger, or more than one. Could it be someone who just looks a hell of a lot like

Beren?"

James shook his head, his expression telling me he felt this was way more unlikely than the other two. "Do you know the odds for someone who already freakishly looks like Beren who also has a vendetta against him?"

"No. But the fact that there would be odds works for me. If there is a chance, however slim, we need to at least consider it."

Will gave me a cautious look. "I kind of agree with James on this one. I think the first two options are the most likely, but I can't pick which one is more likely. Probably the surgery one if I had to pick."

Imani nodded. "Yep. I agree. If there was a spell that could do that, surely we would've worked it out by now. It's pretty much impossible as far as I'm concerned." She tilted her head to the side. "The other angle we haven't covered is that maybe someone just wanted Beren's ex dead and figured they'd frame someone else. An ex-boyfriend would be the perfect person to frame."

James rubbed the back of his neck. "I've seen the statements from her parents and brothers. She hadn't dated anyone seriously after Beren, and she had no other enemies. She was well liked by everyone she met. Her boss was happy with her work, and her colleagues liked her. I didn't pick up on any jealousy or unrequited feelings in any of them." He took a deep breath. "So that brings us back to what we were thinking before. We'll still consider both options, but no matter which one it is, we now need to pull up a list of anyone he's helped incarcerate. Anyone who's ever threatened Beren can go to the top of that list, of course."

"Sounds like a plan, love, and I know just who can help us." Imani smiled.

I grinned at her because I knew exactly who she was going to suggest. "Chad should've been more specific."

Imani's smile widened. "Yes, he should have. I'm sure your mum will be only too happy to pull up the records we need."

James nodded. "Good. We require someone on this we can trust, and there's no one I trust more than Mum. Let's do this. We'll reconvene tonight at Angelica's. We could do with her input on this as well."

Will nodded. "This is her nephew, don't forget. She'll want to cover everything to make sure it wasn't him. If he says it wasn't, she'll believe him."

"He's telling the truth." James's jaw muscles bunched.

Will held up his hands, palms facing my brother. "I know. At least, I don't think he did it at this stage, but all the other evidence so far is damning. Unless we can prove who did do it, we're going to have to concede he had us all fooled." Will drew a deep breath and blew it out. "I'm just hoping like hell that he is the person we thought he was, and we never have to face that hard truth."

Imani stood. "This isn't going to get us anywhere. We have a course of action. Let's just follow it until we reach the end of the road. When we get there… if it's not what we want to see, we'll figure out how to deal with it then. For now, we need to dig. If Beren is innocent, we don't want him sitting in jail."

I stood. "I'll go visit Liv. I'm sure she's beside herself."

Will's forehead wrinkles deepened. "Don't tell her anything, except we're going to try and help. You can let her know we've been banned from the case."

"Okay. Should I ask her to stay over tonight? She probably won't want to be at home by herself and worry all night. I can't imagine she'll get much sleep."

"That's a good idea. And I'm sure Beren will appreciate us taking care of her as best we can." Will gave me a sad smile.

"Okay. I'll see you all later." I magicked my camera home —I did not want any evidence here for anyone to find—and left the room, my stomach gurgling in protest at the constant stress. It seemed like today had been one blow after another. I didn't know how much more I could take before I went to bed and refused to come out. Maybe I should have some squirrel time after I saw Liv. It wouldn't solve anything, but it would help me deal.

Or maybe it wouldn't.

Because the day wasn't nearly over.

There was plenty of time for the universe to land one final punch.

And boy, was it a doozy.

CHAPTER 5

The time had just gone seven thirty, and we had Indian takeaway lined up on the kitchen table as a serve-yourself buffet. Mum looked at me. "Should we start without her, or do you want to wait?"

Angelica, Will, Imani, and James stood around the table waiting for my answer. I grabbed my phone out of my pocket. It wasn't like Liv to be late, let alone half an hour late, but maybe being upset was making her slow? I didn't even know if she'd told her parents about Beren being in jail, but I doubted it. They didn't know about witches, and the last thing you wanted your parents knowing was that the man you loved had been arrested for murder.

"I'll give her a call and see where she is." Liv and Beren lived only a few minutes away, so the hold-up couldn't have been traffic. I dialled her number and listened as it rang and rang. It clicked through to voicemail, and I hung up, then dialled again. This time I left a message. "Hey, Liv. We're waiting for you. If you're going to be longer than another five minutes, can you let me know? See you soon." I hung up and returned everyone's worried gazes. "If we don't hear anything in the next five minutes, I'm going over there."

"I'll go with you, love."

"Thanks." I swallowed my worry. "Why don't you all start eating. You've had a long day, and I know Liv won't mind. I'll eat with Liv when she gets here."

"Okay, then. I'm all for manners, but I'm also practical." Angelica picked up a bowl and spooned rice, then beef vindaloo into it. She was a woman after my own spicy heart. The hotter the better. The fragrance made my mouth water, but being the awesome friend I was, I'd wait for Liv.

Everyone served themselves, then sat at the table. Imani and I stayed standing. I checked my phone. "It's only been three minutes, but why wait? We might as well go over there now and see whether she's left."

Imani smiled. "You're not a very good waiter."

"And this is news to who?"

She laughed. "Okay. Let's go." We stepped out into the hallway, made our doorways, and left. When we arrived at Liv and Beren's reception room, I donned a return to sender. There was no reason we should need to protect ourselves, but my radar was pinging. Liv was punctual and the sort of person who messaged if she was running late. I couldn't brush off her behaviour as being caused by stress.

Imani had walked in behind me, and I pressed the bell. After waiting for a moment, I pressed it again. It was like the phone a few minutes ago—still no answer. I called Will. "Hey, is she there yet? She's not answering the door."

"No. Maybe try her phone one more time. If you don't get an answer, let me know. James and I can come over and disable the magical security." Of course they had spells protecting their place. Lucky he'd reminded me, or I might have broken in, only to have had a freeze spell or something worse accost me. Hmm, but I had a return to sender up.

"Won't my return to sender protect me?"

"No. Since these are created and tied off—it's more like walking into a spider web than the spider web jumping out at you. The magic knows the difference. It would let you get gotten."

I couldn't get my head around how sophisticated magic could be, so I just agreed. There was no use trying to understand it. "Okay, great. I'll ring her and get straight back to you. Bye." I hung up and called Liv. Her phone rang out again, so I dialled Will.

He answered straight away. "We'll be there in a sec."

I relayed the info to Imani, and we made sure we were standing against the door, to give Will and James room to come through. I brought my hand to my mouth and bit my nail. Imani slapped my hand down. "Filthy habit, love."

I narrowed my eyes. "Hey, I'm stressed. This is what I do." I brought my hand to my mouth again, and she hit it away. I needed to chew my nail, dammit. My hand shot to my mouth. I was too fast for her. He he. But as I started chewing, she grabbed my wrist and pulled my arm down. I grunted and tried to heave my arm back to where I wanted it.

Will came through as our tug of war heated up.

"Filthy habit!"

"Give me my arm back."

"What the hell are you two doing?" Will asked.

We stopped and looked at him. "Lily wants to bite her nails. She's old enough to stop such a disgusting habit. It's gross."

"Would you rather I had a nervous breakdown, hmm?" I pinched my lips together and raised my brows.

She rolled her eyes as James came through. "Such a drama queen."

James looked at us, then at Will. Will shook his head in a "don't ask" way.

"Fine, I won't ask. Let's focus. I'll get you two ladies to move to the wall behind me. Will and I need to concentrate. It might take five minutes, but it could take twenty. I helped create the protections, but they're pretty complex."

"Do you want us to leave and come back?" I asked. I didn't want to leave, but maybe it would be easier for everyone if I could bite my nails in private… or at least without Imani scolding me.

James considered my question. "That might be best. Will can call you when we're in. In the meantime, if she shows up, let us know."

"Will do." I made my doorway and left, Imani right behind me. I magicked my key to myself from my bedroom and unlocked the reception-room door. I found Mum and Angelica eating dinner where we'd left them.

They both looked up when I entered. Angelica put her fork down and her poker face on. "Sit. Have something to eat while you wait."

"I'm not hungry anymore." I didn't know what could've happened to Liv, but something was wrong, and not worrying was impossible.

Mum swallowed the food in her mouth. "Just sit, sweetie. Angelica's right. You need to eat. If things go south, you'll need your strength, and you won't have time to eat."

Wow, had she always been so… to the point? Way to stop me worrying, although, to be fair, maybe she knew I was going to stress anyway. She was just telling it like it was. I pulled out a chair and sat. Imani walked in and sat next to me. She reached over and grabbed a bowl and started filling it. "Eat something, love. We might have a busy night ahead of us." She set her bowl in front of her and gave me a sympathetic look.

"Okay." I set my phone on the table so I could check the time whenever the urge came upon me. Then I picked up a bowl and put a samosa and some green-looking yoghurt sauce into it. I had no idea what it was called, but I loved it. We quietly ate, my ears on high alert, listening for Liv's car or her knock.

After touching my phone screen about five times in five minutes, my mother's brow wrinkled. "Lily, stop that. It's going to make the time seem even slower."

I sighed. "I know. I just have a bad feeling about this. What could've happened to her?" I sat up straighter. "You don't think she's visiting with Beren, do you, and just forgot the time?" That would make total sense, and I couldn't believe we hadn't thought of it.

Angelica frowned. "No. He's not allowed any visitors except his solicitor, or an agent interrogating him."

My eyes widened. "That seems harsh. Is that normal?"

Imani and Angelica shared a look. Imani put her fork down. "Usually, when someone's been arrested, they can have one family or friend visitor for fifteen minutes. Chad decided that rule doesn't apply this time."

"What?! He can't just do what he feels like. What a bast—"

"Unfortunately, Lily, he can." Angelica gave me a stern look. "Getting all worked up about it isn't going to help, so just cool your jets."

I raised a brow. "Cool my jets?" Angelica was rarely so… casual with her language. I glanced at my mother. Had her more relaxed style started rubbing off on her? Hmm, weird. "Can you just stick with your normal language? You're freaking me out. I can't take any more changes."

My mother chuckled. "Change can be a good thing. You're too uptight."

"I'm not uptight. Right now, I'm worried about one of my best friends. I was a bundle of relaxed joy before I came here. It's not my fault my loved ones are in danger every five minutes."

"Don't forget you too," Imani mumbled through a mouth half full of food.

Gah, yes. As if I needed that reminder. "Yes, let's not forget Piranha and co." I tapped my phone screen. Eight minutes since we left the boys at Beren's.

Angelica's voice was calm and businesslike. "Those wards could take a while. Please pass the rogan josh, Lily."

I did as asked, then something soft and squishy rubbed against my leg. I leaned down and patted Ted. "Hey, buddy. I don't think you can eat this food. Sorry."

My mum looked at me. "Yes, spicy food is no good for dogs. Besides, I fed him about an hour ago. Don't fall for his sad 'I'm starving' eyes."

Imani smiled. "Dogs are such cons. So are cats, for that matter."

A meow came from the door, and Angelica smiled. "She's taking offence to that, and I don't blame her." She cocked her head to the side. "I never would've thought I'd enjoy having pets again, but I'm not unhappy you adopted those two." Which had been a relief all round. If she'd wanted them gone, Will and I would've had to move out—there was no way I would've fobbed them off to someone else. They were part of our family now.

My phone rang, and I started. My mum gave me a "really?" look. I shrugged and picked my phone up. "Hey, Will. Please tell me you got in."

"Yes, and we need you here ASAP. There's no one here and no sign of a struggle. Her car's not in the driveway. I hate to say this, and I don't know what to make of it, but Liv's clothes are gone from the wardrobe."

"What? Are you implying she's done a runner?"

"Possibly. Could she have gone to her parents to ride this out and was so upset, she forgot to tell you?"

I bit my lip. "Maybe, but I don't think so. And I can't exactly call them and ask. That would just worry them if she isn't there."

"Just get over here and take some pics. Then we'll know whether it was voluntary or not." He hung up without saying goodbye. Why did men always do that? Like that little bit of effort was just too much after having a whole two-minute conversation. I shook off my irritation and told everyone what was going on.

"I'll come with you," Imani said. "I know I don't have to, but you might need moral support. I can't see her ditching us and going to her parents without giving you a heads-up." Which was what I thought. It was too out of character, and I'd seen Liv in more than one ridiculously stressful situation. She'd never lost the plot before.

Mum stared at me with a worried parental face. She was right to be apprehensive. If someone had abducted Liv, I wasn't going to like what I saw, and it would be confronting. I rubbed my forehead and tried to ignore the tightness in my chest and shoulders. I stood. "Okay, I might need it. Let's get this over and done with."

"Good luck, sweetie."

"Thanks, Mum."

Angelica said nothing. She watched me closely, her poker face giving nothing away. Okay, so she was concerned too. Surely she knew I wasn't going to break over whatever was coming. At least I didn't think I was. As long as Liv hadn't been killed, I'd be fine. I'd been through enough to know we'd all band together and figure this out. *There's a first time for everything.* Stupid voice in my head. *Shut up, voice.*

Phone in hand, I went out to the hallway, made my portal, and stepped through to Liv's reception room. I kept walking through the door and into their entry foyer. "I'm here!" I called out.

"We're at the back door," James answered, his voice in the distance. There was a hallway and two rooms between me and the back door.

"I'm going to start here."

"Okay."

Imani came through the door. "You starting from here?"

"Yep. The boys are at the back door if you want to see them."

She nodded but stayed, moving to stand next to the wall, out of my way. I gave her a small, grateful smile and took a deep breath. "Show me Liv, just before she left here the last time."

The light didn't change much. Slightly more evening light coming from outside, and the hall light was on, like it was now. Liv stood at the reception-room door, her back to me. The door was open.

I sucked in a breath, and my heart galloped as if I were running for my life. I snapped a pic, then hurried around to the side of Liv and took a shot of her from that angle. Her mouth was wide open, her eyes round. She couldn't believe it either, apparently. I took a close-up of the man. I didn't know how in the hell he was standing there, but he was.

Beren.

What the hell was going on?

"Lily, are you all right?"

I lowered my phone and stared at Imani. I shook my head. "I don't know. Tell me how to make sense of this?" I handed her the phone.

Her eyes bugged wide, and she jutted her chin out, moving her face closer to the phone. She blinked, then looked at me.

"I know, right?"

She shook her head, then called out, "James, Will, get your arses in here."

Their hurried footsteps echoed through the house. James got to us first, Will right behind. James's alert gaze went straight to Imani. "What is it?" She handed him the phone. He looked at the two pictures. His brow furrowed. "This is impossible."

Will grabbed the phone and stared at it. "What in the hell is going on?"

"Are his clothes here?" I asked.

"I didn't check his wardrobe," James said. I knew they had his and hers closets—Liv had been so impressed when she moved in that she'd sent me a photo when she'd put her stuff away the first time.

Will turned and hurried up the stairs. We waited a minute until he returned. He trudged down the stairs, his face wearing an expression I'd never seen before—baffled. "His clothes are gone too."

James whipped his phone out of his pocket and made a call. "Hey, Gus, it's Agent Bianchi here. Can you quietly check on Agent DuPree and let me know if he's still in his cell?"

James waited a moment, then said, "Okay. Thanks. I'll wait for your call." He looked at us. "I don't trust anyone else to enquire about it."

Imani held her hand out to Will. "Can I see that again?" He gave her the phone. She peered at the side-on photo and enlarged it on Beren's face. "Hmm, I'll admit that I haven't studied Beren that closely, but he doesn't have a scar on his neck just under his earlobe, does he?"

James grabbed the phone. "No, he doesn't." He lifted his gaze to meet Imani's, both of them looking thoughtful. "We're back to our earlier hypothesis. If Beren's still in jail, we know it's not him." He tried to hold his expression in place, but a small smile burst forth.

"Don't count your chickens," said Will.

James's phone rang. "Agent Bianchi here." He listened for a moment. "Thanks, Gus. Yes, please do. No, don't say anything. Okay. Bye." As soon as James hung up, his phone dinged. He opened the message and held up his phone for us all to see. "Here's Beren, where we left him."

Beren was lying on his bed, arms behind his head. He was looking at the camera. For someone in jail for murder, he sure looked calm. Maybe because he knew he was innocent, and he believed in us. My stomach flipped, and I swallowed the nausea threatening. "If Beren's in there, who has Liv?" Before, our hypothesis was so far out there because Beren could've done it, but he couldn't be in two places at once. Who was his doppelgänger, and what did he want with Liv?

Will's brow furrowed. "The million-pound question. One we need an answer to ASAP."

"Did you look for magic signatures?"

James looked at me. He hesitated before answering. "We found one upstairs, at Liv's wardrobe."

"Why didn't you tell me?"

Will put his palm on my back in a soothing gesture. "We didn't want to worry you more than necessary. We haven't had time to send it for analysis yet."

"I'm going to go and run it now," said James. "I'm not going to trust anyone else with this information."

"What do you want us to do?" Imani's back was straight, and she was almost on her toes, ready for action.

"Let Ma'am know what we've found and wait for me to come back. I think it's urgent that we find out who has it in for Beren. I want you all going over those files."

I pressed my lips together. "But Bad Chad said you're not to have anything to do with it. How are you going to get those files home?"

Will gave me an "are you kidding" look. "Duplicate them with magic and bring them home. As if he's even going to know. Quite frankly, Lily, I'm disappointed in your lack of imagination on this one."

James tapped my arm and handed my phone back. "Just before I go, can you confirm it's not Beren?"

I knew what he meant. "For sure. Hang on." I called up my magic and pointed my phone at the doorway. *Show me the last time Liv was here with Beren.* Morning light shone into the hallway. Beren was in his PIB uniform, smiling at Liv, who was smiling back. I clicked a shot. He definitely didn't have a scar, and if this was in the morning, it definitely hadn't been him here this evening. I showed everyone the photo. "It proves it's not him."

Will smiled. "That's brilliant. What would we do without your talent?"

"Thanks. The only problem is, we can't prove it to anyone else." I frowned. I took a deep breath. "If we can't clear Beren the old-fashioned way, we'll have to use these."

James set his mouth in a hard line. "No way, Lily. I won't put you in more danger. You've only just got your life back."

"You don't know for sure that I'll be targeted. But we do know for sure that B will stay in jail forever if we can't prove his innocence."

Imani held her hands up. "Just stop. We don't have time for this now. Liv is with this guy, and we have no idea what his intentions are. Come on. We have to solve this quickly." She was right. Liv's life was in danger. Did she realise it wasn't Beren? Had she gone willingly? Surely not. She would've called or messaged… unless he'd convinced her, as Beren, that he'd already told us he was taking her away.

"I'll see you back at Angelica's in the next ten minutes. It won't take long to run the magic signature through the system and grab the files I need. Be ready to work." He made his doorway and left.

Will's magic prickled my scalp. It was more than what was needed to make a doorway, so I asked, "What are you doing?"

"Looking for evidence." He watched the spot Beren's double had been standing in my photo. He held out his palm. "Place any evidence left behind by the man who took Liv into my palm." Imani and I stared at Will's palm. It was as empty as before the spell. He shrugged. "I had to try. Come on, let's go."

Imani locked the reception-room door, and Will made a doorway and gestured at me to step through. As soon as I was out the other side, I went through the open reception-room door—looked like Imani hadn't bothered locking it when we came here the second time, which was fair enough. She knew we might be in a hurry when we returned. I headed straight for the kitchen.

Angelica and Mum were sitting at the table, their cups of tea in front of them. Dinner was gone, but a cheesecake sat in the middle of the table. Mum smiled. "I thought I'd whip this up. None of you ate properly. The leftovers are in the fridge if you'd prefer."

"Thanks, but I'm not really hungry right now." I pulled out a chair and sat as Will strode in. I magicked myself a cappuccino because it was going to be a long night.

Mum gave me a hopeful look. "It's lemon. Your favourite."

I looked at the cake and bit my lip. I hated rejecting something Mum had made. She wanted to be nurturing, and I was taking that away from her. But I had to be true to myself too. This parent-child thing was difficult when I wasn't used to it. After everything she'd been through, the last thing I wanted was to make her sad, but if I explained it like that, she'd get annoyed and cranky with me. It had happened three times in the last week, so I decided to keep it to myself. I'd just have to live with the guilt. "Maybe later. We have a lot to tell you."

Imani walked in as I unlocked my phone and slid it across the table to Mum and Angelica. Imani sat. "Lily's not wrong. Maybe you could sum it up, Will."

"My pleasure." He started by telling them everything we'd found and not found, then finished with an update on what James was doing.

Angelica stared at the picture, unblinking. What was going through her head, I couldn't say. This was her nephew—probably her favourite one. I had no idea if she had any other nieces and nephews, but she worked with Beren and spent lots of time with him, which had made them close. She finally looked up from my phone and donned her best poker face,

Ma'am mode activated. "Have they gone through the car yet?"

Will shrugged one shoulder. "They'd started, last time I heard, but now I'm out of the loop. We've all been banned from working on the case, not that that's stopping James grabbing the info we'd been gathering about who could hate Beren enough to do this."

Angelica lifted her chin. "Yes, well, Chad's kept me busy with other work, and I no longer have the authority to give myself different cases." She drained her teacup and magicked it away. "I really ought to do something about him. He has to go."

I smiled. "I would love to see that."

My mother's face grew serious, and she levelled her gaze at me. "Be careful what you wish for."

Angelica put a hand on Mum's forearm. "It's okay, Kat. This has been coming for a long time, and the situation with Beren has just proven how vulnerable we all are while those who are in charge remain there. I agree that today is not the day to push forward, but that day is soon coming. I think it would behove us to start planning as soon as we solve Beren's case."

What the hell was going on? Yes, we'd been having trouble with Chad and the directors for ages, and Angelica went missing for a long time, and it was all to do with those dynamics. But whether she'd been investigating or lying low, she never told us. And what would happen when she went after them?

Angelica looked at me. "I can see the hamster wheels turning in your head. When we start down the path of cleaning out the PIB, it will be even worse than RP. If we're not ready, we'll pay the price many times over. I wanted to

WITCH NEMESIS IN WESTERHAM

wait, but they're forcing our hand." My mother gave her a worried look and licked her bottom lip. Had Angelica been letting Mum in on everything she wouldn't tell us? Was that why she'd brought her back to work?

I rubbed my forehead. Would the drama and risks never end?

A knock sounded on the reception-room door. I jumped up, the screech of my chair drilling into my head. I winced. "That must be James. I'll get it." Sitting at the table while Liv was missing, plus hearing we were heading into even more trouble gave me the jitters. If we didn't have so much work to do, I'd put my runners on and head out. My nervous energy could easily power five miles.

I unlocked the door and swung it open. James stood there, his arms full of folders. I moved aside and let him hurry through before he dropped everything—not that he couldn't magic everything back in order in five seconds. Old habits died hard.

After locking the door, I went back to the kitchen and sat. James stood at the head of the table and magicked the files around, placing a couple in front of each person, including himself. He sat. "I checked in on B via security camera. I couldn't talk to him, of course, but he's definitely in his cell. At this stage, I don't want to tell him about Liv because he's already told us everything he knows about anyone who'd have it in for him, and I don't want him worrying until we better know what we're dealing with. It's a matter of us going through these files and using the process of elimination." His magic tickled my scalp, and a laptop appeared in front of him. "We'll start by confirming whether our suspects are living or dead—some of these files haven't been updated for two years." Beren was not going to be happy when he found out James had kept Liv's disappearance from him, but I could understand why he had. Beren would be helpless from jail, and he'd only feel more guilty for ending up there in the first place, even though it wasn't his fault. I sighed to myself at how bloody unfair it all was.

Angelica shook her head. "Sloppy reporting. The bureau's been on the slide for quite a while." She opened her file. "I'll go first with my list. You can cross out the ones who are dead." Her magic tingled my scalp, and a small pile of papers appeared in front of James. Looking at my own papers, I could see that one person was on each page. It stated name, date of birth, last known address, a small mugshot photo, and other details, including what they'd been charged with and convicted of. What a stellar bunch of crims I had. The first one had poisoned his boss when he wouldn't give him a raise. Another man magicked his wife to the middle of a nearby lake, knowing she couldn't swim. Apparently, she'd panicked and couldn't figure out how to make a doorway around herself to return. She'd died. A twenty-year-old woman had magicked some jewellery and Apple products from the shop when her parents refused to get them for her—not super bad, but it was her third offence, so she'd landed six months in jail. I doubted she should be on our suspect list. And there were five others I needed to research. Yikes. So many criminals. "Beren's done a great job in his career. Look at all these people he's helped put away."

Angelica nodded. "As my nephew, he's had to work harder to prove himself. Neither one of us wanted anyone to think he received special treatment. He's a hell of an agent."

My heart constricted. "Do his parents know what's happened?"

Angelica looked to James. My brother cleared his throat.

"No. We haven't had a chance, and Beren didn't want to. I doubt Liv's parents know either."

Imani turned her gaze on Angelica. "Ma'am, don't you think they should know? Surely someone will want to ask them questions. Better they find out from you than Chad."

"I'm not going to tell them tonight. They can have one more night of peace. I'll tell them in the morning. I want a night to sleep on it as well. Going to them with no answers is not good enough. My brother is like Beren—he's a sweet man. He's not going to cope well, I'm afraid. They check in with him every second day, to make sure he's okay because of his job. When he moved here from London, they almost followed him, until he convinced them he'd come over once a week for dinner." She stared into space for a moment before shaking her head. "John and Valerie just wanted to be parents, and they came into it later in life, but they've always been grateful for Beren."

"He's still alive though." I didn't want to be mean, but it wasn't as if he'd died.

"Yes, dear, I'm well aware."

My cheeks heated. "My point is, it's not the end of the world, and we're going to get him out of this."

"So we hope." She looked at James. "Have you finished yet?" Wow, she was being snitchy with him too. Other than the obvious, what had gotten up her nose? She'd been dealing with things just fine until we'd mentioned his parents.

Will put his hand on my leg and gave me a "don't worry" look. I gave him a "what else can I do?" look.

My mother jumped in before James could answer. Her voice had a low level of fake cheer. She turned to Angelica. "Oh, I just thought of something. Do you remember that case with that exceptionally gifted make-up artist? She worked with her husband and disguised him as all manner of different people, usually famous people. Their likenesses weren't identical, but they were pretty good. Her husband swindled tens of thousands of dollars from people by getting free stays at hotels, free dinners, or the promise to come back and pay later. We caught him when he was pretending to be Sir Michael Parkinson and trying to drive off with a brand-new Jag. The dealer wasn't impressed by who he was and called us."

"Ah, yes. I remember that." Angelica's mouth quirked up at the side. "He'd been served by one of the young salesmen and would've gotten away, but the manager was watching from his office, and he was a witch, so when the thief tried to magic suggestions to the young man, the manager came down and cast a don't-move spell. We later explained it away as an unusual form of epilepsy where the person freezes."

I smiled. "That's quick thinking by everyone. Very cool." I looked at Mum. "So, you think whoever this is might have a very clever accomplice?"

She nodded. "It's possible."

Angelica made an "I'm not convinced" face. "That takes such a great level of skill, the likes of which we haven't seen in the twenty-seven years since."

"Just putting it out there. You know we have to consider all angles."

Angelica's poker face returned. "And we are."

"Here." James leaned over the table and handed Angelica her papers. He held out his hand for my mother's. Gah, I was dying to take Imani and Will aside and ask if they knew what was up Angelica's bum, other than the obvious. I'd never seen her so off-kilter.

Beren slowly updated everyone's paperwork, and then we silently worked through them. After an hour and a half, we'd eliminated about a third of the initial suspects. I flicked through the pile and counted thirty suspects. "Sheesh. This is a lot of people. And we've likely missed a couple who might hate him, even though he hasn't arrested them."

James sighed. "Yes, it's a lot of people, but it won't take long to whittle them down. Two-thirds of them are in jail, so I have easy access to question them, and I'll use my talent to figure it out. If I find the guilty party, we'll need to dig for evidence, of course, but if we can get a direction tomorrow, we might even find Liv by tomorrow night."

"That's best-case scenario though." Thanks to Will for being such a realist. Hope had started to edge into my chest, but it fled at his words, and my shoulders slumped. Why did he have to be right?

"What about the ones who aren't in jail?" I asked.

"We'll have to bring them in for questioning." James looked at Angelica. "How do we get around Chad? I really want to be there to suss out any lies."

Imani put her hand up but didn't wait for acknowledge-ment before she spoke. "I think you can trust Agents Smith and Singh, and they're already involved, so it won't look strange."

Angelica nodded. "I agree. They're definitely on our side, and we can trust them to keep mum to Chad. We might also want to cause a distraction to make sure he isn't around when those suspects are questioned." She looked at my mum. "Are you up for the challenge?"

Mum grinned. "Always."

Will's gaze pinged from Mum to me and back again. He smirked and whispered, "So, that's where you get it from."

"What?"

"Your cheeky nature. You love stirring things up."

I smiled. "You know it." My smile fell. We'd need to do more than stir things up if we wanted to find Liv. Damn these witches and their stupid doorways. Yes, I was a witch, but I'd gladly give up doorways if we could track Liv right now and save her. The stinging heat of frustration needled my stomach. I stood quickly, my chair scraping torturously against the floor. Imani cringed. "Sorry."

"Are you all right, love?" she asked.

"I'm just… argh. I'm finding it hard to sit here and do nothing."

Lines appeared on her forehead. "But you're not doing nothing. You've just helped us narrow down a suspect list."

"Yes, but it feels like nothing. Liv could be dead by now." I swallowed against the need to throw up.

Will grabbed my hand and looked up at me. "She's not dead. I have a feeling whoever wants to torture Beren will want to let him know she's alive and at his whim." He tugged my hand until I sat. He looked at Angelica. "That's what we can expect, isn't it?"

Her serious gaze met him squarely in the eyes. "Yes. I wouldn't be surprised if he somehow gets a message to him in jail. But it's a tricky situation. If this is about revenge, which I think we can all agree on at this stage, he'll want proof of Beren's tortured reaction."

There was something I didn't understand. "But how will he even know if his message has reached Beren, let alone see his reaction. I mean, what if the PIB decides not to tell Beren about Liv?"

Will's gaze landed on me. "I'm sure he'll have a plan. Maybe he'll hand something to someone who doesn't realise Beren's in jail. Anyone who meets him who knows Beren will think it's him."

Imani tilted her head to the side. "Hmm, should we be on the lookout around headquarters for his doppelgänger?"

James tapped the tabletop. "Maybe, but surely he wouldn't be so stupid?"

Mum raised a brow. "If this person has the skills for disguise we think he does, he could easily pretend to be someone else. We'd never know. Judging by Lily's photos, he'd fool any of us. He could turn up looking like Chad." She made a good point… a scary point.

Fortunately, we still had one advantage. "At least he doesn't know we know that he's a master of disguise." I wasn't sure how that would give us an advantage, but at this stage, he had no idea we knew how he was able to get access to things like Beren's car. He could've easily spied on Beren at work or gone through his stuff. No one would've realised. "Does anyone think he's probably been following B for a while? I mean, how else would he know where his car was kept? And I know his address isn't listed anywhere because he's an agent. How would this person know where he lives?"

Imani nodded. "He's probably been following B and definitely Liv when she's left headquarters in her car."

Angelica smoothed a hand over her immaculate bun. "He might even have walked straight into headquarters and had lunch with Liv for all we know. If he has mind-wiping abilities, there's no telling how often he's interacted with her." This was getting scarier by the moment. Angelica's magic tickled my scalp. Six rings appeared on the table. Plain bands, each about a centimetre wide. "We used these pinky rings on another case, ages ago, so our undercover agents could recognise each other in the field. If we each wear one, we can make sure our target can't pretend to be one of us."

"That's a great idea." Will reached out, took two rings, and passed the smaller one to me. He slipped the other on his pinky finger. His gaze flicked to Angelica before landing on James. "If he's targeting Beren's loved ones, we probably should tell his parents ASAP and put a protective ward around their house." Wow, he'd purposely avoided aiming that question at Angelica. How she'd take that, who knew, but I'd bet we didn't have long to find out.

James took one of the rings and put it on. He quickly looked at Angelica, then back at Will. "That's a good idea. Is there anyone else we need to worry about?"

Will shook his head. "Just us, but that's neither here nor there. I doubt we're targets, and even if we were, that's life as normal, isn't it?"

James smiled. "Yep."

"Isn't anyone going to ask me what I think?" Angelica had one eyebrow raised. To be honest, she'd shown massive restraint not weighing in until now.

James stared at her, his poker face hiding what was probably a war within himself to defer to her and go against what he believed was right. It didn't take a genius to know that as experienced and hard as Angelica was, one of her most beloved family members was stuck in the middle of this, and her judgement might skew the wrong way because of non-law-enforcement considerations. If this were anyone else, she would've told their parents already and protected them. He finally said, "What *do* you think?"

She folded her hands, rested them on the table, and lifted her chin. "My thoughts haven't changed from before. This might be the last good night's sleep my brother gets for a while. I do, however, agree they need protection, which is why I'm going to travel to their reception room and sit there. No one can get to them unless they travel to their reception room or are buzzed in from the street. I can hear if anyone buzzes, as their reception room is near their foyer. And if anyone tries some kind of nasty spell from outside, I'll feel the magic and be able to throw up a protection spell."

James took a deep breath and let it out. He gave Will a look. My brother was smart enough to know when he was beaten. He looked at Imani. "Do you mind accompanying Ma'am? You can take shifts."

"It would be my pleasure." Imani smiled. Her magic tingled my scalp, and a rollout mattress appeared on the floor next to her. A pillow sat in her lap. "I'm ready." She looked at Angelica. "I'd grab a pillow for yourself, but we can take turns on the mattress. I take it there's a chair in the room?"

She nodded. "Yes, dear, of course there is." Angelica looked at James. "I'm glad you can see I'm right."

"Always." His slight smile showed there were no hard feelings. When dealing with Angelica, it was best to leave your ego at the door. My brother had years of experience with her, but he was also a good guy. Her idea was the next best thing to throwing protection spells up. She and Imani would be in a small amount of danger, but nothing serious enough to warrant upsetting Angelica and her brother. His gaze shifted from Angelica and Imani to Will, Mum, and me as he spoke. "While you're there, we'll research the suspects who are out and about, see where they're working, living, etcetera, and first thing in the morning, I'll call Agents Smith and Singh, and get the interviews happening." He scratched his eyebrow, then looked at Angelica again. "When you've spoken to Beren's parents, please let me know."

She gave a single nod. "Of course." She stood and turned to Imani. "You can go first." They both said goodbye; then Angelica made her doorway, and they left. We spent the next few hours grabbing every piece of information we could, but we ran out of leads just after three in the morning. As much as I was worried about Liv, I fell asleep almost as soon as I dropped into bed. Which was a good thing because I had a feeling tomorrow was going to be exhausting.

I wasn't wrong.

CHAPTER 6

The next morning, Will left at eight. I got up, too, because worry about Liv had me staring at the ceiling. Getting back to sleep wasn't an option, so I magicked clothes on and went downstairs to the kitchen. It was my job to feed the animals, and right on cue, Ted met me at his bowl, tail wagging. I gave him a pat and a hug, then magicked homemade food into his bowl. It was a mushy concoction of rice, vegetables, and meat—his favourite, so he'd conveyed to Will. Abby was the lucky recipient of chicken thigh fillet and chicken livers. Mmm mmm. Yeah, nah. Seriously, I knew so many people wanted to come back as a cat, but the eating of cat food was enough for me to say no thanks. Add to that licking their own butthole, and I was definitely out. Being a squirrel was where it was at. I was pretty sure they didn't lick their own bottoms because I'd never seen one do that. I'd have to google it and check, just to make sure. Wow, how low I'd fallen when that was my plan for the day. I shook my head.

"Hey, sweetie."

I turned and smiled. "Morning, Mum." I gave her a hug. "You're up early."

"So are you. I'm betting you're even more worried than I am?"

"Probably." I frowned. "If anything's happened to Liv…."

She squeezed my forearm. "Angelica called me this morning. The night was uneventful, but she's told her brother, and he rushed straight to the jail. His mother had to be sedated."

I blinked. "Yikes. That's awful."

"Yes. Angelica called her sister-in-law's best friend to come sit with her, and now Angelica and Imani are back at head-quarters."

"Hopefully Chad won't get in the way of what they need to do."

"Yes, we can hope. I'm going in soon. I start at nine."

"Hmm, how do you fancy breakfast at Costa?"

She smiled. "Sounds good."

We wandered up there, ordered, and nabbed a table at the back of the café. I hated when the window seats were taken, but these were better than nothing. At least I had Mum to talk to today. Most times, I was here by myself because everyone was at work. Now that RP were no more, I was going to concentrate on getting more photography work, and I'd decided to make landscape shots a priority. Even though I had Angelica's car to drive whenever I wanted, it was time to get my own car. I had plenty of savings, and since I was going to live here, I might as well. I hated being indebted to people, and buying my own car was one step in the direction of my inde-pendence.

We sat, and I licked the chocolate foam off the top of my

cappuccino before grabbing my chocolate muffin and taking a good old sniff.

My mother, who had a coffee and a ham-and-cheese toastie in front of her, shook her head. "Must you be so uncouth?"

"What? I'm enjoying every aspect of my food. It smells as good as it tastes—it's all part of the ritual."

"Surely I raised you better than that?"

"Hmm, maybe…."

She shook her head, but a small smile invaded her face. "It is good to see you all grown up. There were many times that I'd given up on this ever happening."

I reached across the table and grabbed her hand. "I never did."

"And you have no idea how much I appreciate that." Her eyes glistened. Before mine had the chance, I slid my arm back to my side of the table and changed the subject.

I made a bubble of garble, which was kind of like a bubble of silence, but it just made what you were saying unclear to those around you. Will had taught it to me the other day. How it was that I was still learning common spells was beyond me. It was embarrassing, really. "What about your magic? If we could figure out a way to bring your future-telling skills back, we could possibly find Liv sooner." I wasn't sure how Mum would take my question, but it was something I'd come up with on the walk over here. She hadn't spoken much about losing her magic, and as far as I knew, she wasn't game to see if she could get it back, just in case it wasn't possible. I guessed having some hope, no matter how infinitesimal, was better than having none.

Her brows drew down, and she looked at her food. "It won't work. He burned me out, Lily."

"Maybe I can help?"

She lifted her head and looked me in the eye. Adrenaline-laced guilt shot through my stomach. Anger heated her gaze and gave her words a searing edge. "You can't help. You don't think Angelica's tried? My magic is just as elusive today as it was the day you rescued me. Every time we try, it's excruciating—both mentally and physically. And you want to put that guilt and pressure on me to try and help Olivia? Don't do that to me, Lily. You, of all people, should know better."

My cheeks burned. "I'm so sorry, Mum. I didn't mean to upset you. I just thought—"

"No, you didn't think. That's the problem." She shook her head and stood. "I've lost my appetite. I think I'll go to work early."

Crap.

I was about to say goodbye, but she didn't give me a chance. She turned and hurried to the door. Then she was gone. I breathed out a huge, angst-ridden sigh. How had it all turned so bad so quickly? The guilt of hurting her warred with my indignance that my friend needed my help—and we weren't talking help choosing a dress, for goodness' sake. Her life was in danger, and my mother didn't care. Surely she could've just said no without the drama? Maybe my request had given her a panic response? I shook my head. If only she'd let me help her—Olivia or no Olivia. If I was honest, it rankled me that she didn't trust my abilities. What if I was the one who could help her, and she would never know because she thought me incapable? I felt terrible for hurting her, and I'd apologise again later when she'd cooled down, but I had no idea what I was going to do about her treating me like a child. Could it be that when she left, I was a normal person, and after so many years, suddenly I'm a witch? Our roles had been reversed in a way. Was she struggling with that too? Maybe she was still just so damaged from her ordeal that she couldn't offer a more balanced approach right now? I sighed. I would remain patient until we figured it out.

Except, some things couldn't be fixed. I hoped our relationship wasn't one of them. Yes, we were both way older than when I'd last seen her, but I didn't remember her being so quick to anger. She'd been so kind and loving when I was a child. Bloody Dana and her father. They'd changed her, and she wasn't entirely the mother I remembered. But at least I still had her, and I'd do my best to make it up to her. Maybe she just needed time?

I looked down at our food. My mother's appetite wasn't the only one that hadn't survived the argument. I finished my coffee and requested a paper bag to go, then placed our food into it, and left.

As I walked home, my phone rang. Hmm, no caller ID. I was tempted to ignore it because it was probably some scammer telling me I was going to be arrested for tax fraud and I should call the tax department and pay my bill. But what if it was Liv who'd managed to get to a phone when her kidnapper wasn't paying attention? "Hello?"

"Good morning, Miss Bianchi."

"The voice was kind of familiar. I narrowed my eyes. An American accent. It must be my "favourite" living person. How rude of him not to say who he was. Time to play dumb. "Hello? Who is this? If you're a scammer, I'm going to hang up. You have five seconds to explain who you are and why you're calling me. And do you know how boorish it is not to introduce yourself when you call someone? So ill-mannered." I think I'd gotten enough insults in there. I stifled a giggle and snorted.

"Oh, it's Agent Chad Williamson the Third, the head of the PIB and your boyfriend's boss." Wow, so many titles, just in case I wasn't sure.

"Oh, Chad! I know who you are now. Sorry that I didn't recognise your voice. It must be forgettable or common or something." I might be pushing the frenemyship, but I needed cheering up, and annoying him would totally do it. I could imagine his face turning red right about now. I grinned.

"You're the forgettable one; not me. Such a useless civilian. I have no idea why that DuPree woman ever started getting you to help."

His insults were so third grade. Amateur. "In that case, I guess you probably called me by mistake. Check you later." I hung up before he had a chance to reply. If he wanted a favour, which I was guessing he did, he'd call back, but in the meantime, I'd gotten to hang up on him. I chuckled. Playing with Chad was ridiculously enjoyable.

As I reached Angelica's, the phone rang again. "Hello?"

"We seem to have gotten cut off."

"Who is this?"

He took a few seconds to answer. His brain probably needed time to reboot after short-circuiting. I was pretty sure the slight muffle to his voice was because he was gritting his teeth. *He he.* "It's Agent Chad Williamson the Third."

"Oh, hi. How are you?"

"*Fine.*" Oh, he was totally gritting his teeth. "You need to come in and see me."

"I do? I can't imagine why. No offence, but you're the last person I want to… oops, I mean *need* to see today. Plus, I'm busy." Well, okay, so I hoped I had offended him. If he wanted to ask a favour, bossing me around was not going to get it.

"Be at my office in ten minutes, or your boyfriend gets it."

My mouth dropped open, and rage boiled in my chest. What the hell? "You can't threaten to kill Will! You touch so much as a nose hair, and I'll—"

"Don't be stupid. I'm not going to hurt him, but I will fire him. I'm looking to unload some employees, and he's first on my list. Ten minutes." He hung up.

He might be an idiot, but he was still dangerous in some ways. I supposed Will could always get a job in the French office since Chad didn't have authority over them. We could move to Paris, although we wouldn't even have to move since we travelled everywhere. Maybe we could have an apartment there—paid for by the PIB of course—and stay there a couple of nights a week. Hmm....

But in the meantime, I had to go see that pathetic excuse for an agent.

I opened the front door and went inside, curiosity overcoming my anger at being ordered around and threatened. I'd get him back. He was going down as soon as I figured out how. Lately, there'd been too many distractions, but some of our angst had been his fault. And now with Beren in jail and Liv missing, he was a big, fat, moronic obstacle in our way to fixing things. Why the directors had him in there was another question. From what I could gather, Angelica had the support of only one of those directors. Were they planning a coup?

I shook my head, clearing the chatter. All this speculation would get me nowhere, and it was sucking valuable brain power from what mattered right now—finding the killer and Liv, and freeing Beren. When the time was right, we'd get rid of him. Sadly, that time wasn't today. Bummer.

Hmm. All wasn't lost for today though. He hadn't cared when I said I was busy, as if everyone had to bend to his will immediately. And I didn't much like being ordered to do something, especially not from someone I despised. So, I was going to make this as ridiculous as possible. Let him try and have a serious conversation with me. Maybe he'd rethink ordering me to help him.

When Mum came to live with us, I'd helped clear space in the built-in wardrobe in her room. I'd discovered an awesome bumble-bee costume. Angelica wouldn't admit to ever wearing it, and I didn't blame her—it was round and huge and very yellow and black, and I didn't know if any of us would quite fear her as much if we could've imagined her in it. But it was perfect for me to wear to see Chad. As much as my heart hurt for B, and my stomach was a cauldron of acidic worry, dressing up would help take my mind off things I could do nothing about in the super short term. Plus, angering Chad would go some way to cheering me up. I could pretend for an hour that the only thing I had to worry about was Will's idiotic fool of a boss.

I magicked the costume on with black tights and black sneakers. It had wings, a stinger, as well as a cap that tied under my chin, antennae attached. I was round and furry, silly and cute. Chad was going to hate it. Which meant that it was perfect.

I grinned and made my doorway to headquarters.

Let the fun begin.

I buzzed the intercom. When Gus answered it, I was laughing because of my pun. He stopped mid hello, a "what the hell" look on his face. Then he grinned. "Miss Lily, lovely to see you. Can I ask why you've bumbled in here today?" I mentally applauded his pun. I should've known he'd be a punner. *Punners are funner.* I chuckled.

"Hey, Gus. Someone ordered me in here, and I want to be a thorn in his side…" I turned and wiggled my bottom, revealing my stinger. "Or, rather, a stinger." As he moved out of the way, I squeezed through the door. Wow, this costume was really round. If I fell over, I'd probably be unlikely to get up without help. Note to self: don't fall over.

"The wings are a nice touch."

"Why, thank you." I shimmied my shoulders, moving the wings.

Gus shut the door, and I shuffled quickly along the hallway, making bee noises. "Bzzzzzzzzzzzzz."

"Wait for me, Miss Lily." Gus jogged to catch up. An agent I didn't know was walking towards us. His eyes widened when he saw me. I smiled, and he shook his head. Gus gave him a serious nod as we passed. "Morning, Agent Priddle."

"Morning, Gus." He side-eyed me and hurried away. Gee, it didn't take much to scare some agents.

We hopped in the lift, and up we went. I turned to Gus. "How's B holding up?"

He frowned. "I think he's okay, but I haven't seen him today. They're keeping me busy. I did a couple of hours at the front entry, scanning security tags and making sure no unauthorised weapons enter the building." The doors opened, and we walked down the hall. "Last night, he was okay. He's unhappy and worried about Miss Olivia and how she's coping, but he has a quiet confidence, which I'm assuming is because he knows his mates have his back."

"We certainly do, Gus. We certainly do." My chest tightened at the pang of worry that hit me. At least Beren was safe where he was, but Liv…? I looked down at my round bee belly —at least it was cuter than a beer belly. But, seriously, what the hell had I been thinking? Maybe all this stress was making me a little crazy. Possibly after this, I could sneak down and try and cheer B up. A bee for a B.

"Aaaand, we're here."

I blinked and stopped short. At least getting stuck in my head made for quicker travelling time. It's like when you hop in the car and half an hour later arrive at your destination with no clue as to how you got there. Automatic pilot was handy, if not a little dangerous. "Thanks, Gus."

He gave me a serious look. "Good luck."

I smiled. "Thanks, but he's the one who needs it." I winked, hoping to make my lie more believable. Chad didn't normally call me in to see him. The last time was when he banned me from headquarters, and that had gone swimmingly. What in the world did he want? I hated not knowing stuff. Things were much easier to deal with if you knew exactly what you were dealing with. Hmm… at least I knew I was dealing with an idiot.

Gus opened the door and announced me. As I slipped past him and he shut the door, Chad flicked a glance to me, then looked back at his phone—he was typing, maybe messaging—then he did a double take, his eyes widening. I grinned. He placed his phone on the table. "What the heck are you wearing?"

"Oh this?" I looked down at my costume and ran a hand over the fuzzy expanse of belly. "This is my bee costume." I pulled out a chair as if everything was normal and tried to sit. It was rather awkward because the costume was so round. With some effort, I managed to jam myself in between the arms. Hopefully I wouldn't be stuck later when I tried to get up.

"I can see that. Why in the heck are you wearing it here?"

My face was all innocence. "Why not? Bzzzzz." I bit my tongue to stop the laugh trying to explode from my mouth.

That buzzing was such a great afterthought. Moments like these made me proud to be me.

"Why not?!" His nostrils flared. "Because you're disrespecting the establishment and the boss of everything."

"The boss of everything? Who's that?"

He slammed one hand on the table. "Me!"

I stared at him and ran a finger up one of my antennae, then played with the blob on the end. The antennae was attached to the cap with something firm and springy, so that when I pushed it down and removed my finger, it sprung up. Cool! I did that a couple of times, just for fun. "What do you want? I have things to do this afternoon. I'm a very busy bee. Bzzzzzzzzzzz." The smile I gave him couldn't be any sweeter if I'd tried. His face couldn't have been any angrier. Telltale red stained his neck and travelled upward, like a thermometer on a hot day.

"You a—"

"Bzzz." I quite enjoyed buzzing. Maybe my spirit animal wasn't a squirrel. I might have missed my calling as a bee. Could I be a hybrid squirrel bee? Cute, furry, nervously scurrying but one who could do the buzz noise, plus have a stinger on the end of my tail? Or would they make me a kind of bee/squirrel/scorpion hybrid? Hmm….

His brows rose, and he clamped his lips together. Anger level rising. It was at his chin now. "Don't interrupt!"

"Sorry. I'll try and bee-have. See what I did there?"

He blinked, and wrinkles embedded in his forehead. He probably didn't get the pun—it was above his intelligence level. What a waste of a good pun. He ground out his next words with his back teeth jammed together. "I detest you. If it were up to me, you'd never be allowed here ever again. In fact, you'd be locked up with your friend downstairs." *Ooh, tell me how you really feel.*

"Bzzzzzz." That one was for Beren. God, I hoped my brother was getting some info with those interviews.

"Dammit! Stop being absurd and listen." The reminder of Beren had taken some of my buzz away, so I shrugged. Prolonging this wasn't in my best interests. The less time I spent in Chad's presence, the better. Might as well get it over with. "Good. Now, would you like a drink? A water, tea, coffee?"

"Have you got any herbal tea… something with flowers in it?"

He blinked slowly, possibly thinking, but who knew? Maybe his brain just turned off for a moment and he was rebooting. "No, we have none of those airy-fairy drinks here. If I had my way, I'd get rid of all the tea. The agents around here have way too many tea breaks. It's just an excuse to slack off, if you ask me."

"B—" I just stopped myself from buzzing, otherwise this could go on all day. And why was he being decent all of a sudden, asking if I wanted a drink when he clearly didn't like people having them on the job? My eyes wanted to narrow in suspicion, but I kept them in check. If he was being dodgy, no sense in letting him know I was onto him. But how he thought he'd bypass my bull-crap radar is beyond me. This civilised behaviour was extremely sudden.

He smiled. I shuddered. His fake smile was more predatory than friendly. I checked my return to sender was up. It wasn't, so I made one with the slightest magic. Hopefully he hadn't felt it—I didn't want to alert him to the fact that I knew some-thing was going on. Thankfully, the return to sender didn't use much to create it—it was just using it that took all the effort and power. And not that I thought he would attack me, but my gut told me to be on alert, and if I did anything right today, it was going to be listening to my gut... my very big, very round bumble-bee gut.

He sat forward and clasped his hands, resting his forearms on the table edge. "I hope we can talk frankly, Lily."

Hmm, this should be interesting. "Of course." I gave him my best serious face, which must have looked ridiculous with my headgear, and wings poking over my shoulders. And no matter how silly I was, Chad was sillier if he thought he could fool me for even half a second. I fought the smile tugging at the corners of my lips. If only someone were videoing this. I'd love to watch it later.

"Well, as you know, Angelica and your brother have been involving you in some of our investigations."

I waited for him to continue, but he was waiting for me to nod. Eye-roll averted by sheer iron will, I nodded. My smile this time couldn't be contained when I felt my antennae wobbling around in the aftermath.

He smiled in return, probably thinking I was keen to hear more. Idiot. Maybe his new name should be Chadiot? Hmm, not sure about that one. It didn't sound quite right. He really needed a good nickname. "Are you listening to me?" His brows drew down, and his hands squeezed together.

"Oh, sorry. Um, please go on." Ha! I could annoy him even when I wasn't trying. I mentally high-fived myself.

He cleared his throat a bit too enthusiastically, making a really gross noise. I cringed—if he wasn't going to be subtle, neither was I. "As I was saying... you've been involved in a lot of investigations. I need you to tell me what's so special about you."

"Is this what you needed when you called me?" That's a

weird thing, ordering me to tell him about myself. It didn't gel with the phone call. This wasn't really doing anything.

"Not exactly, but it's a start. So, tell me."

I tried to cross my arms over my chest, but the costume bulged too much. I rested my arms on the chair arms instead. "I have good observation skills." His chin dipped down, and he gave me a "yeah, right" look. "Seriously. Being a photographer, I have to observe closely. I see things others don't."

He leaned back in his chair and steepled his fingers, just like Dr Evil from the *Austin Powers* movies. All he needed now was a fluffy white cat. "Forgive me if I say that I don't believe you. There must be more to it than that?" I shook my head. As if I would give away my secrets that easily. He was delusional if he thought I would ever trust him. His lips pressed together briefly. "Come on, Lily. You don't expect me to believe you don't have some kind of special talent that your brother and Angelica find useful?"

I shrugged. "Believe me or don't. I really don't care."

He narrowed his eyes. "Right. We'll come back to that. The next thing I want is for you to tell me about Angelica. What she's been up to in the last few months." He must've seen the incredulous look on my face because he added, "I just want to make sure she's okay. Her behaviour hasn't been… stable lately. I think some of the directors have concerns about her ability to serve. If there is any reason you can think of, I'm sure they can take it into account and rethink her demotion."

My eyes widened. "Demotion? She's already been demoted. Are they going to have her cleaning toilets or something?"

He waved an arm casually and fake laughed. "No, of course not. We might give her a leave of absence for a few months, see if she can straighten herself out."

"But she hasn't done anything wrong."

"She's insubordinate. She risks her life and the agents she works with every time she decides to do her own thing against orders. Do you want your brother, and partner to be at risk because of her arrogance?"

I sighed. "Do you really believe the crap you're spouting? If anyone's dangerous to the safety of PIB agents, it's you."

"How dare you!" He slapped both hands on the table, the *crack* vibrating throughout the room. It took all my will, but I refrained from jumping, and I gave him my best bored face.

I tried to stand, but my costume was jammed in between the chair arms. Damn it. My attempt at a smooth exit was ruined. I wriggled and grunted, and finally the thing popped free. I smoothed my hands down my black and yellow fuzz, then looked at him. "Well, if that's all you want, I'm out of here. This was a colossal waste of my time. I would never ever tell you anything about Ma'am if I thought it would hurt her. Try someone else."

"Even if I fire your brother and William?"

I'd call his bluff. They could both get a job in France. The job security would be way better. Since we'd linked up with the French office, Chad's threats weren't as scary as they used to be. The boys had choices, and so did Angelica, but I figured she had so much history here, and it would break her heart to see it disappear in a flaming pile of poo. Not to mention the safety of millions was at risk if the English PIB office disintegrated. What was the board of director's endgame? "Yes, even if you fire them." I wasn't going to skite about where they could go after here because he'd try and find a way to stop it. Not that he could do anything, really, but why risk it? I pushed my chair out and moved to stand behind it. "Now, if you'll excuse me, I have plants to pollinate, honey to produce."

His eyes widened. "How dare you! I haven't dismissed you yet. As soon as you're gone, I'll be calling in your brother and William and firing them." He smirked and folded his arms in front of his chest. "How do you like them apples?"

"I prefer flowers, actually." I wiggled my bottom and showed him my stinger. "Bzzzzzz."

His mouth pinched in horror, his nostrils flaring as he drew in an enraged breath. He jumped to his feet and, again, slammed both hands on the table. "I will not be made fun of!"

"Ah, you finally get it." I smiled. "It's about time. I was beginning to worry my insults weren't hitting the mark." I had nothing to lose since he was going to fire them now.

"You will tell me what I want to know!" He stood straight and planted his hands on his hips. "You. Will. Tell. Me." His face was so red, he might be about to blow a heart valve. This should be interesting.

"No." I smoothed my tummy fur and smiled.

"Yes!"

I magicked a piece of paper and black marker from home. I stepped to the table and drew a big *NO* on the paper and held it up, giving him a grin. "You can read, can't you?"

A malicious smirk twisted his face, and his magic prickled my scalp. Before I could react, he whispered something, and a spell hit my shield. I stepped back a pace, my stomach aching slightly before the sensation disappeared and it was as if nothing had happened. I cocked my head to the side. He still looked the same. What had he tried to do?

"Tell me what your special talent is, and tell me what Angelica has been doing the last few months. You will also spy on Angelica for me."

Had he thrown some kind of truth or compulsion spell at me? That was so illegal but totally unsurprising. I drew my power and stared at his aura. It looked like it was a compulsion spell. How could he have no idea it had been thrown back to him? Hmm, maybe because until you feel the compulsion, you might not notice it's on you? Did the spell hitting him just feel like he was casting a spell? Could he have been confused? Whatever it was, he was a total idiot, but I could use it to my advantage. "Okay, I'll tell you." My mouth dropped open in faux surprise that I was actually telling him. "Clues stand out to me, as if they're shining bright. I can go to a crime scene and pick out the physical evidence straight away. My other talent is that I can tell when someone hasn't washed their hands after going to the toilet."

His brow furrowed, and his gazed dropped to his hands. He folded his arms, burrowing his hands under his armpits. I smirked. Busted.

"I can also tell how high someone's IQ is. I'm sorry to tell you that yours is… hmm… not great. I'm honestly surprised you landed this job over Ma'am, who is far superior to you in every way. Really, with your… limitations, you should be doing a job that requires far less thinking." If my logic was working, it stood to reason that now he had to tell me what I wanted to know, but in doing so, he would surely realise what had happened. All it would take was for him to check my aura properly. Did I want to get info right now, or did I want to feed him false information? And how long did that spell last? If he wanted me to spy on Angelica, it was probably a long-lasting spell. If it was long-lasting, I could always get the info later.

Decision made.

His hands were still on his hips, and he stomped his foot. I snorted. "I am not stupid! I got this job because I'm awesome."

"Aha, yep, sure. You tell yourself that."

He strode towards me, stopping two feet away. He pointed a wobbling finger at my chest. "You're not very nice. And you haven't told me about Angelica. Where was she when she disappeared?"

"I actually don't know. She didn't tell us where she went. And lately, as far as I know, she's just working the assignments you give her."

He narrowed his eyes, probably assessing whether I was lying, but then his face relaxed because he probably remembered he'd spelled me. Ha ha. Stupid witch. "And you're sure?"

I rolled my eyes. "Of course I am. Can I go now?"

"No! You have to promise to spy on her."

"Okay, I promise."

His eyes widened, but then he smiled. *Yes, Chadiot, the spell.* If the directors wanted Angelica's demise so badly, why had they put this moron in charge? Maybe there was no one better they could trust to do what they wanted? Or maybe he was just weak. A stronger person with any sort of morals already working as an agent would likely have the PIB's best interests at heart… except for the RP recruits. Hopefully we'd weeded them all out, but you never knew. "I want you to check in with me every couple of days. I'll call you and order you in when I'm ready."

I laughed, and he laughed along with me. *I'm laughing at you, not with you, Chadiot.* That lame nickname would have to do until I figured out a superior one, but it was better than Chad. "Can I go now?"

He nodded. "Yes."

I gave a nod, pretended to fly to the middle of room as I buzzed, made my doorway, and left. That was probably the silliest exit from the conference room ever, and I was proud.

What a complete and utter moron that man was. And why was he demanding all this information now? I also wanted to go back and see Beren, but I wasn't sure how I'd hide that Liv was missing. He was likely to ask me how she was.

I let myself in with my key. Voices came from the living room. It sounded like Angelica… and James? Excitement at spilling what had just happened zinged in my veins, pepping my step. I chuckled at the rhyme as I entered the living room.

James and Angelica were, indeed, there, as was my mother, Will, and Imani. James stopped talking. He, Mum, and Angelica were facing me. Their eyes widened. Imani and Will, who'd been sitting on the Chesterfield opposite them, stood and turned. Imani's mouth dropped open; then she burst out laughing.

Will sniggered. "What in the hell, Lily? Have you been out in the garden pollinating?"

I laughed. "Ha ha, I wish. I've been collecting something even better than pollen."

Angelica had the faintest of smiles. "Do tell."

My brows drew down. "How come you lot are having a meeting without me?"

James ran a hand through his hair. "Sorry, Lily. We didn't think to call you."

"As soon as you don't need my special skills, you cut me out? That's not very nice, considering Liv and B are my friends too."

Mum frowned. "Sorry, sweetie. You're right. We should've called you, but we thought we were being nice by leaving you to whatever it was you were doing. We thought you might be out and about, taking photos or something." Hmm, it seemed she was willing to put the morning's argument behind us. At least that was something.

"Okay, whatever. Just let me know next time. Okay?"

James nodded. "Okay. So, where have you been, dressed like that?"

"Chad called me in for an urgent meeting, and I thought I'd dress special for the occasion."

"Oh my God, love!" Imani held her belly and laughed loudly.

My declaration even elicited a grin from James. "What? I wish I'd been a fly on the wall." His grin dissolved. "Why did he call you in?"

I walked around the couch because this discussion was likely to take a while. I sat on the other side of Imani, who was now in between Will and me. I accidentally bumped her with my bee body. She pushed me, and I squished between her forceful hand and the chair arm. Time for the costume to go. I patted the black and yellow tummy. "It was nice bee-ing you." I drew my magic, and the costume disappeared, jeans and a T-shirt replacing it.

"That's better, love. Are you kidding that you sat through a whole meeting dressed like that?"

I smiled. "Nope. It was hilarious. Chad is such an idiot too." I told them everything that happened, from "go" to "whoa." When I finished, everyone sat there, mulling. "Does anyone want a tea or coffee?" I asked. Okay, so I didn't have to because food and beverages were a finger click away when you were a witch, but old habits….

"No, thanks, Lily," said Will. James and Angelica nodded in confirmation of Will's statement.

"Okay, cool. Just making sure." I magicked a cappuccino to myself and took a sip. Mmm, so good. With Beren in Jail and Liv missing, plus the weirdness with Chad, it was as if I was standing outside being bombarded by a hailstorm, but cradling the warm cup in my hands, inhaling the sweet, earthy aroma, it was as if a protective cocoon had wrapped around me. Time stopped for a few moments as I savoured the coffee infusion.

Angelica pinned me with her gaze, dissipating the cloud of relaxed ambiance I floated in. "Lily, we'll have to talk about you spying on me tomorrow. I'm going to come up with some falsehoods you can tell him—that's assuming his superiors don't see that spell tangled in his aura any time soon. But that whole situation is… interesting. I'm sure we can use it to our advantage. At least it confirms what I've suspected for a while. Chad is definitely working for someone who's determined to get rid of the old guard, the trustworthy agents. Whether it's to shut us down or create some kind of criminal organisation with an honest front, who knows? Anything could be going on right now."

"Angelica's right." James wriggled his bottom to the edge of his chair and leaned towards me. "I've done over twenty interviews so far, and none of them are our guy. I have to go back out this arvo." He didn't need to say why—because Liv's life was in danger. Damn it! Why couldn't we work this out quickly? Who hated Beren enough to do this to him?

James's phone rang. "Agent Bianchi speaking." His mouth opened slightly as if he was going to talk, but he didn't. His eyebrows rose. "Right. Okay. We'll come in now. Has anyone notified Chad?" He nodded. "Okay, good. Keep it that way as long as you can. I'll see you in five. Bye."

"Who was that?" Will asked.

"Beren's solicitor. One of the guards called him in after Beren found a note in his cell a little while ago."

Angelica stared at James. "A note?"

"It's probably from the doppelgänger. And I have no idea

what it says yet. Mr Royston said it contained a threat, but he didn't give any specifics." He stood and looked at Will. "Come with me. I want Angelica out of this as long as possible. The last thing we need is Chad coming in and telling her to keep out of it."

"Yes, indeed." Her tone was dry. "I want to have another chat with his parents. There's something we're overlooking. I have that niggling feeling."

My mother touched Angelica's shoulder. "I can come with you."

"That would be lovely. Thank you."

I looked at James. "Maybe I should come with you? Do they know who passed the note on? Maybe I can take some pictures? And does this mean B has a road out? Doesn't it prove that he didn't do anything, that he's been targeted and set up?"

James shook his head. "Not necessarily. It depends what's in the note."

Imani nodded. "Agreed, but I do think Lily's got a good idea there. I'd like to think we can rely on video footage, but just in case…."

James rubbed his forehead, likely thinking. After a while, he said, "Let us do this first. We'll find out if anyone saw anything. If we come up blank, we'll call you. In the meantime, you've got another case to work on, and we don't want to draw Chad's attention if other things aren't getting done."

Imani sighed and stood. "Fair enough. I'll get going, but call if you need me."

"Will do."

One by one, everyone made their doorways and left, Will giving me a kiss before joining my brother. I sat back on the couch as Abby came around the corner of it. "Hello, kitten. How are you?"

She rubbed against my leg and purred. *Fine, thank you.* I sucked in a breath. Huh? Was that a thought or a feeling or a voice? I wasn't quite sure. I stared at her, my heart racing.

"Did you just talk to me?"

She jumped into my lap and gazed up at me. Her mouth was turned up in a… smile? She meowed again. *Yes, I'm talking to you. You can understand me, finally! Honestly, I thought it would never happen. You get in your own way too much.*

I looked askance at her. Was I imagining this? Had B and Liv's predicament pushed me over the edge? "I get in my own way?"

"*Meow.*" *I'm hungry. Can I have some tuna?*

"Are you kidding me? I finally understand you—I think, unless I'm going nuts—and it's so you can ask me for food?"

And, that is a problem, why? It's about time, really.

"You had breakfast. You're going to have to wait for dinner." She leaned back on her hind legs, lifted a paw, reached up, and smacked my cheek with it. It was soft yet a tad aggressive, although she hadn't used claws. My mouth dropped open. "Kitty-bopping me isn't going to get you fed. In fact, I could give you tinned cat food for dinner rather than the fit-for-human kind. How would you like that?"

She narrowed her eyes and did a growly thing low in her throat. *I think I liked it better when you couldn't understand me. You were much nicer then.*

I shrugged. "If I could turn this off, I would. Now it's here, I'm not sure how to shut you out." As overjoyed as I was—boy, had I been waiting a lifetime for this ability—it was also an "oh no" moment. This could be a bad thing. Now Abby could beg me whenever she wanted, and I'd feel guiltier for saying no. Rejecting the request of a meowing cat was much easier than a talking one. Best not to say anything. I wasn't giving the enemy a sword to cut me down with—her claws were sharp enough.

You don't want to shut me out—you love me. There was a distinct smugness in her thought.

"Yes, I do love you." I lifted her so her paws were resting over one of my shoulders and rubbed my face against hers. "You're so soft and warm." She purred, and I smiled. That was more like it.

My phone rang, and I started, not expecting anyone to call so soon after they'd left. At least I was pretty sure it would be one of my agent friends because I didn't really know anyone else here, and my Aussie friends were likely asleep. Also, Chad had already called me today, and he supposedly didn't want me again until the day after tomorrow. I slid Abby to my lap and answered the phone. "Hey, James. What happened? Is everything okay?"

"Not entirely. We need you to get here ASAP. Gus is ready for you. Come straight down to lock-up and bring your phone." His agitation came through loud and clear, which made my nape itch. He was usually so calm, even in a crisis. This obviously wasn't good. Crap.

I assumed he wanted that for photos. I was a genius. "Okay. I'll see you in a couple of minutes." He hung up as soon as he had my confirmation. I gave Abby a hug goodbye, placed her on the couch, and stood. After sliding my phone into my pocket, I made a doorway to the PIB reception room.

Gus answered the door when I buzzed. He kept his voice low, subdued. "Hello again, Miss Lily. Twice in one day."

"Yes, it's becoming a habit."

He quickly shut the door and led me the opposite way to

WITCH NEMESIS IN WESTERHAM

normal, to the lift that went to the cells. We didn't talk. What-ever had happened must be serious… or at least Gus was worried we might come across Chad. I didn't have the energy to ask. Fear of what was going on made my mouth dry and my brain busy.

The lift's descent seemed to take an eternity, and I shuffled from foot to foot until it jerked to a halt at the bottom and the doors opened. Gus motioned for me to get out first. After I exited, he took the lead again until we were at the security entry to the jail section. A heavy steel door set with magical wards barred our way. My hands sweated, and I swallowed the iron tang in my mouth. Memories of my time in here smacked me in the gut. It wasn't so much the physicality of being locked up but the fear of not knowing if I would be convicted of crimes and be imprisoned indefinitely. It also brought back the sadness and terror of not knowing what had happened to James.

But it had all turned out okay in the end. I had to remember that more than anything. It would be the same this time… wouldn't it?

Gus pressed an eight-digit code into the panel on the wall. Nothing happened straight away. We waited. Eventually, magic tickled my scalp, and the door opened. James was on the other side. He gave a worried look to Gus. Gus shook his head, then turned to me. "In you go, Miss Lily. I'll be here waiting for you." He gave James a wink.

"Thanks, mate," my brother said while standing aside for me to slip into yet another hallway. The door shut behind me, and James looked at me. He made a bubble of silence. "You'll have to be subtle with this one. We'll be doing everything in front of the security cameras."

"What *are* we doing?"

"The note given to B disintegrated as soon as he read it. It's basically a fine dust on the floor. We've bagged it, but there's no way we'll get any evidence from it. It's ingenious, really, because the magic signature broke into infinitesimal pieces with the paper."

"What? That's crazy."

"I know. I've only ever heard of that happening one other time in all my years with the PIB, and it sucks. It means that all we have is Beren's recollection of what was said, and he's not sure how accurately he's remembering it because he was in shock at the message."

My stomach clenched. "Liv… is she…."

"She's still alive, but… well, just come and take a photo."

"How can I use my magic down here? Isn't it blocked for most people?"

"Yes, unless you have a special code for a spell that creates a kind of exclusion zone around a witch. It has to mesh with the blocking spell that's already here."

"And you know that code, of course?"

He smiled. "You bet."

"Okay, well, that's better than a kick up the bum."

He raised a brow. "Indeed, it is. Come this way." He turned and walked down the corridor to another room, which had eight TV security screens, a witch guard watching them. James gave him a nod.

The guard was probably mid-fifties, with thinning blond hair, short beard, and a neck tattoo. My heart skipped, then beat forcefully. *Gah, calm yourself, Lily. It's a red rose, not a snake.* I swallowed and took a deep breath. The guard smiled at James. "Back so quickly?"

"Yeah, mate. Gathering the troops." He winked, and the

guard turned his swivel chair so he could look at me. "This is my sister, Lily."

I waved. "Hey. Nice to meet you."

He smiled and gave me a nod. "Nice to meet you too. I have the utmost respect for anyone who had to grow up dealing with that rapscallion." He grinned.

I grinned in return. "Thank you. Your sympathy is appreciated."

The guard looked at my brother. "You'd best get in and do whatever it is. My shift change gets here in thirty minutes."

James nodded. "Understood." He gazed at me. "Come on."

My brother went to the only other door in the room and punched numbers into the wall-mounted panel, and the door clicked open. He nudged me through and shut it behind him. "Okay, before we go any further, I'll cast your little protection bubble."

"Sounds cosy." I lowered my voice. "By the way, can you trust that guy?"

"Yep. We go way back, and he's an Angelica supporter. He's done things for us in the past that prove his loyalty. Let's just leave it at that."

"Fine with me." I would always trust my brother's judgement —his special lie-detecting talent gave him an edge that other people didn't possess, and by other people, I meant me. The number of times I'd met someone, gotten to know them, and still been duped was embarrassing. Hmm. It was probably safer if I avoided new people for a while. Now that I could talk to animals, they could keep me company instead. Would Costa let me bring a therapy squirrel inside? This bore further investigation.

"Lily?"

"Oh, what? Sorry."

He shook his head. "Yeah, yeah. Off with the squirrels again."

"How did you know?"

"You're really going to ask me that."

I smiled. "Okay, I take it back."

"I was saying, let's get started. Are you ready?"

I interlinked my fingers. "As I'll ever be."

James's magic prickled my scalp, and the scent of rain filled the air. Okay, weird. Pressure built, and it was as if I were being slightly squashed by full-body memory foam. The uncomfortable sensation lasted for roughly fifteen seconds. Then it disappeared. I rubbed my arms and body, checking everything was normal, then I waved my arms in a wide arc, testing the air. It seemed as it was when we'd first come in. Interesting. "Is that it? Do I have a protective magical-access bubble now?"

He smiled. "Yep. Now, when we go in there, I'm going to let you into the cell with B. Just do what you have to quickly and get out. He's going to sit where he was when he read it so that if anyone sees the video, they won't think it's weird. Andy in there will stop the recording, just in case, but I want to make sure. Someone could even walk in."

"Covering all bases is smart. Let's not slip up and give Chadiot a chance to fire you and Will."

Conversation over, he led me through one more door and into a corridor that contained the holding cells. We walked past a vacant one, then two occupied by beefy males, inked to the eyeballs… in fact, one had those tear drop tatts just under his eyes. I shuddered. Beren was in the fourth cell we came to.

He quickly sat up and swung his legs over the bed. The haunted look in his eyes broke my heart. Tears burned my eyes, but I blinked them back. He needed us all to be strong. The chances of him wanting to cry were high, and the least I could do was not blubber and make him feel worse, considering he was holding it together. Instead of crying, I smiled. "Hey, B."

James unlocked the cell door, and I hurried in and threw my arms around Beren. He returned my hug and squeezed tight. I didn't need to ask how he was to know he was hurting. The question would be a waste of time, so we just hugged. Eventually, we pulled apart. "Boy, am I glad to see you." He shook his head and ran a hand through his messy blond hair. "My brain is all over the place, and I can't remember exactly what was in that damn note. It roughly translates to, "I hate you, I have Liv, and I'm going to play with her for a while before I kill her, and then I'm coming after everyone else you love."

I clenched my fists at the hatred and gall of the evil witch who'd done this. "Jesus. Who hates you that much?"

He shrugged. "I've given a list to James and Will."

James made a bubble of silence and placed a gentle hand on Beren's shoulder. "And we're working through it, mate. I'll be going out with Will later to finish up on interviews."

"Thank you. So, what now?"

"I'll get you to sit on the bed again, roughly where you were when you opened the letter."

I got my phone ready. "Who delivered it?"

James's forehead wrinkled. "He woke up with the letter next to him on the pillow."

I sucked in a breath. "Crap. They got in here? What about security tapes, and how did they get past the guard and security?"

"That footage has mysteriously disappeared. We're chasing

up the guard who was on duty at the time. He's a witch as well, which should've made it harder to get in."

"I'll take some photos for that as well, then."

"Of course." I almost got my back up with that comment, but I remembered just in time that James was under massive stress too. Maybe he thought I was smart enough to know what was needed, which I should take as a compliment.

"Let's do this." I stood next to Beren and pointed my camera towards his lap. I whispered, "Show me the letter from Beren's doppelgänger." A piece of white A4 paper appeared in past-Beren's hands. I took a photo. Straightening, I turned towards the steel bars. "Show me the person who delivered the letter." A man with brown hair in a low ponytail and glasses appeared, the white missive in his hand as he opened the cell door. I swallowed. Crap. *Click*. I handed my phone to James. "I don't suppose the guard who worked before Andy has a pony-tail and glasses?" The uniform was a dead giveaway.

James jammed his teeth together, his jaw muscles bunching. He swore. My eyes widened—he didn't swear often. After looking at both photos, he handed the phone to B. "Here."

Beren stared at the photo with the note for a long time, maybe committing the words to memory so he could mete out justice later. He flicked to the guard pic quickly and handed the phone back to me. "Now what?"

James put one hand on his hip and rubbed the back of his neck with his other hand. "I want to consult with Will. We're not supposed to be investigating this, and questioning a PIB employee who could be charged with colluding with a criminal without any proof? And even if we had proof, we're not supposed to be doing anything." I took a huge breath.

Beren put his elbows on his thighs and rested his head in

his hands while James stared at the floor, thinking. I pulled up the photo of the note and read.

Dearest Beren, brother of mine,

For the first time in my life, I am truly happy. I've killed your ex-girlfriend just so you know I'm serious—I'm sure you still held a candle for her. I imagine it hurts to know she's dead and it's all because of you.

My girlfriend loves me, and soon your, or should I say my, parents will too. I am going to take everything of yours and make it mine, as it should always have been. After years of torture and mistakes made by others, I am getting the life I should always have had. It's only fair, after all. It's your turn to suffer as I have.

As long as Olivia pleases me, I will let her stay. Maybe I'll kill her when I tire of her, but if you like her, I'm sure to, as long as she doesn't upset or disappoint me. In any case, know that I am and always will gloat that things have finally been rectified. Enjoy jail, brother. It's where you belong for stealing my life.

My mouth dropped open. What. The. Actual. Hell? I rubbed my forehead. "And you really have no idea who this could be? Do you have any cousins or siblings you don't get along with?" He'd never mentioned siblings, but maybe he'd had a falling out with one and therefore never mentioned them?

Beren didn't bother looking up, so his voice came out muffled. "No. But I am adopted." Oh, wow. That was something I didn't know. Angelica must know, though. Maybe that's why she was looking a bit cagey at dinner last night.

James sat next to Beren, the bed creaking under their combined weight. "Now that we have the note, I'm going to speak to Angelica. I'm not sure what to do about the guard situation yet. We'll work it out. I promise."

Was James just going to ignore the fact that Beren could possibly have a brother out there somewhere, or was he going to process it and talk to Angelica about the possibility because he didn't want to upset B any more than he had to?

Oh. My. God. The similarities between B and the guy in my photos. Did Beren have an actual twin? No way. That would be crazy. Surely his adoptive parents would've taken both boys. Who would split identical twins up? Beren's parents seemed to be well off. Surely they could've afforded to take both?

James put an arm around Beren and pulled him into his side for a moment; then he released him and stood. "Hang in there. We'll be back later this arvo. Okay?"

He looked up at James, then me. "Okay. And I really appreciate this."

"Don't be ridiculous. You're family, B. Helping you, helps us. We miss you, and I bloody well want my best friend back. If they've hurt her, I'm going to make them suffer."

He nodded. "I would, but…." He motioned to the cell.

"Just leave it to us. We've got this." I sat and gave him a quick hug before joining James on the freedom side of the door. James pushed it shut. The clang echoed through the concrete-floored room and shook my heart.

Beren's gaze slid off us and onto the floor at his feet. My throat tingled, and tears threatened again. Leaving him here by himself with his fears for Liv was the hardest thing I'd had to do in a very long time. I grabbed one of the bars caging Beren in with one hand, wanting desperately to tell James to open the door and leave me here with him for support, but that was madness. If Chadiot found out….

As James's footsteps clacked towards the exit, my hand dropped from the bar. I breathed hopelessness in and exhaled frustration.

Then I turned my back on Beren and followed James out. I knew we couldn't stay there all day, and by chasing things up, we were being more of a help.

So why did I feel like the worst friend ever?

CHAPTER 7

We went straight back to Angelica's after seeing Beren. James called Angelica and Will to meet us there as soon as they could. Thankfully, we didn't have to wait long before we were sitting on the Chesterfields, my mum also in attendance. Imani had gotten caught up with another case, but we'd fill her in later.

James gave them the rundown of what we discovered at the jail. He started with the guard first and ended with the letter. I wondered at the order of things until he addressed Angelica directly. He'd kept his own counsel about the whole thing while we'd waited for everyone to arrive. I hadn't had a chance to discuss the twin thing with him. James didn't beat around the bush. "Is it possible James has a twin, and they were adopted to two different families?"

Her poker face assumed its position. "How do you know about the adoption?"

"He told me ages ago, but he told Lily today, which jogged my memory. It honestly hadn't crossed my mind until then. I was too busy focussing on how someone could make them-selves look like him, not considering that they could've actually been born that way. You have to admit; it makes perfect sense."

Angelica stared him down for what was the longest minute ever. But my brother was one of the most patient people I knew. He calmly waited, his demeanour relaxed, expectant of an answer he already knew. Angelica adjusted her bottom on the seat, as if she couldn't get comfortable. She sighed, possibly resigned? "We asked him not to tell anyone he was adopted."

I lifted my top lip on one side as if to say "huh?" "But why would you do that? It's not a bad thing."

Her chin tilted up, and she looked down her nose at me. It probably wasn't on purpose—just a go-to reflex when she felt threatened. I'd known her long enough that I could sometimes spot a small chink in her normally uncrackable shell. "We don't make our private business public, dear. As far as my brother and his wife are concerned, he's theirs. There are other more personal reasons too. Wrongly or rightly, my sister-in-law feels great shame that she couldn't have her own chil-dren. Bringing the adoption up just makes her feel like a fail-ure. That's all I'll say on the matter."

"Oh, okay. It's sad that she feels that way. For what it's worth, she's an incredible mother. Beren is an amazing human, and it's all because of your brother and his wife. They should be proud of themselves."

She took a deep breath. "I imagine they are proud of that, but nevertheless, it's something they don't like to talk about, and I'm afraid that this suggestion of a twin will only compli-cate matters for them."

James pinned her with his gaze. "So, do you think it's possible? Do you know the circumstances of the adoption?"

Angelica wasn't ready to give in just yet. "Before we get to that, have you interviewed all the suspects?" I went to great lengths to protect those I loved, but apparently, I had nothing on Angelica. This was to the point that it could help them more than hinder them. Surely their pain could be pushed aside for something this important? She must know, but maybe she needed to reassure them we'd tried every other avenue before we'd pushed along that one.

James shook his head. "No. I'll finish them today. Then will you consider what I'm asking?" She didn't answer, but her lips pressed together in a hard line. James stared at the ceiling, maybe looking for more patience. He looked back at Angelica. "We can't question that security guard yet. He has no idea we know, and we want to keep it that way for as long as possible. Plus, we can't tell people how we knew it was him, and Chad has forbidden Will and me from investigating this case. I wouldn't put it past him to refuse any evidence we collect just because. And the longer this takes, the more danger Olivia is in." By the time he'd finished, his eyes had a spark of fierceness that suggested he wasn't going to give in until he got what he wanted. "You know I can look for those records myself. It might take a lot longer to get the information, but I'm willing to do what it takes. I can't believe you'd put your brother's comfort above saving the woman your nephew loves." Yikes. That escalated quickly. As much as I respected Angelica's reasons, I couldn't respect her choices right now. My brother was right. It would be a shame if he had to steamroll over her wishes, but he'd do it, and the rest of us would back him on it.

Angelica's hands sat clasped in her lap. Mum placed her hand on top. Her voice was gentle and coaxing. "It's a hard decision, but you know there's no other way. Do the right thing now. James is right; we can't risk a few hours. Even with that information, it's going to take time to find this man. I feel for your brother and his wife, I do, but how will you feel if something we do or don't do is the difference between finding Olivia alive or finding her dead?"

Angelica looked at my mother but said nothing. If the wheels were turning in her head, I couldn't tell. She abruptly stood, dropping my mother's hand. "I'm sorry, but I have something to do before I make up my mind." Without waiting for acknowledgement, she hurried to the middle of the room, made a doorway, and left. My shoulders slumped. This was crazy. Liv was somewhere being tortured for all we knew, and Angelica couldn't bear to hurt her brother's feelings? An emotional sting is way less horrific than dying. How could she not admit that?

Will and James shared a look. My mother sighed. "I'm sorry she's being difficult. Family… it's hard for her."

James shook his head. "Don't worry. Give her a few minutes. She's normally the first one to do what's right and logical over what's preferred from an emotional standpoint."

Will could obviously see the look on my face. He put his arm around me. "She'll come back and do the right thing. I wouldn't be surprised if she's gone to explain things to her brother. From what Beren says, he's a good guy. There's no way he'd want us to hold back on this for his sake."

"But what about for his wife's sake?" I asked.

Will shrugged. "I don't know, Lily, but let's give Angelica fifteen minutes. If she's not back by then, James and I will go complete those interviews, and we'll get Millicent to start searching the adoption records."

Hair rose on the back of my neck. I shuddered. "We can't

WITCH NEMESIS IN WESTERHAM

wait. If Angelica doesn't tell us what she knows, we'll be too late. I just know it."

Wrinkles embedded in my mother's forehead. "You sound so certain."

"I feel certain. It's probably just me being worried, but…" I jumped up, went to the window, and gazed out at the driveway and row of trees growing along the fence line with our neighbours. "My gut's unsettled."

"Your gut?" James's voice held a note of amusement. "Are you just hungry, as usual? Why don't you go grab a chocolate muffin from your favourite coffee shop?"

"Ha ha, very funny."

"It's not one of your talents, sweetie."

"I know." I hugged myself and made a decision that might affect the rest of my life, but I knew it would make things happen faster for Liv and Beren. It would be worth the sacrifice, and besides, no one knew for sure what would develop when my secret was out. I turned around to look at Will and James. My mother's back was to me, but when I started talking, she swivelled around and met my gaze. "I'm going to tell Chad my secret. We need the PIB's support to find Liv quickly. If Angelica won't help because of an overblown sense of duty, I can't just sit here and do nothing, or do something only for it to all be too late."

Will stood, his expression firm. "You can't do that, Lily."

I folded my arms. "Why not? It's my secret to tell or not."

The worry he'd been hiding behind his bossiness shone from his eyes. "You can't put yourself in any more danger. Aren't you sick of running and living in fear?"

"I won't be running or living in fear. Not everyone is going to freak out when they know. Maybe we can tell him and spell him so he can't tell anyone else on pain of death?"

My mother gasped. "You can't do that, Lily. That's illegal."

James stood and came over to me. "None of us want you to do that. There's another way."

"What way? I'm listening."

James ran a hand through his hair. He put his hands on his hips and again looked at the ceiling. How was *I* trying his patience? I was giving him an out, a way around Angelica. Eventually, he looked back down at me.

Will stayed where he was, but he said, "James, tell her."

James turned and they exchanged a look. So many looks that I knew nothing about. So annoying. If only I could read their minds. At least my mother looked equally as perplexed. "Yes, James, tell me."

He turned back to me and rubbed his forehead before meeting my eyes. "There's a group… an underground society of witches."

Nervous warmth spread through my chest. Not again with the nefarious groups. "Oh my God. Of course there is. And I suppose they're worse than RP, and they hate witches with my particular talent?"

His mouth quirked up on one side. "Not quite, but close. They're a powerful group who tend to stay in the background, but we suspect they've murdered witches and threatened others. Their agenda is to protect witches from humans and from other witches."

"Huh? Now you're losing me. Isn't that the PIB?"

"Not quite. That's what they tell recruits they're doing, and for the most part, they just watch and live their lives, but the witch heading the group is a paranoid narcissist. He's amassed a lot of wealth and followers, so it's almost a cult, but not quite. The followers live their own lives, but if their esteemed leader calls on them to do something, they do it."

"I still don't see how that affects me." The birds chirped outside, their song joyful and innocent, as if we weren't having a crisis in here. If only I could be a squirrel. I resisted the urge to turn and look at the trees wistfully. So many great hiding places where no one could find me and bug me... or kill me.

"The crazy guy who runs it, Roderick Vanderhousen, has a fair amount of power, but he's not the most powerful witch I've ever come across. He recruits witches with less power than him so that he can lord it over them, but he's far from harmless, and we suspect he has artefacts he shouldn't. He follows an ancient way of witches, sort of like an out-there witch bible. It gives witches lists of dos and don'ts, what should be tolerated and what shouldn't. On top of that, he's added his own narcissistic spin on it by declaring that any witch with more than two strong talents should be killed, and on top of that, if a witch comes into this world with the capability of linking other witches or taking power from other witches, they should be killed too."

I swallowed. "Okay, so that's me, but that wasn't the talent I was going to admit to."

Will spoke, his tone grave. "He's particularly interested in any witches with future-telling talents, but there is no one I've heard of who can tell the past as clearly as you. Some witches have a talent of reading an object, but they can only get a sense of things, never actual pictures and proof. I agree with James that this guy would be more than curious if word got out about your talent. This guy uses his talent to stay on top."

I cocked my head to the side. "And what talent would that be?"

James licked his bottom lip. "Truth telling. He's like me— he knows whether someone is telling the truth, and he won't hesitate at breaking down your mental barrier to read your mind—illegal or not, he does it, but his followers don't press charges, and others he's butted heads with, well, a few of them have turned up dead, but we can never pin anything on him. If he found out about you… you're a direct threat to him, not to mention everything else."

I shook my head. "But it's still just one person."

My mother stared at me. "One crazy person. Honey, he was on our radar years ago. He's a dangerous man."

I still wasn't convinced. "But how does he know what goes on at the PIB?"

Will stared at me. "He has his minions, just like RP did. He keeps his radar out for anyone he perceives as a threat, and if rumours got around to his followers of the presence of a witch with your talents, he would act, if for no other reason than to show them he's to be feared and respected. There's no way he'd hear information like that and do nothing."

"He can't afford to," James agreed.

I folded my arms. "Well, according to James, he's not super powerful. So if he attacks me, I'll kill him, and we'll keep on with our lives."

My mother sucked in a breath. "Lily!"

"What? Isn't that how I've dealt with most other bad witches who've tried to kill me?"

"Is it?" Her eyes were wide.

James looked at her. "I'm afraid it is, but Lily had every right." We hadn't filled Mum in on everything that had happened while I'd been here—we didn't want to worry her after the fact. She knew about a couple of incidents, but not everything. Maybe that's why she didn't fully appreciate I was a capable adult and witch. James looked at me. "You probably could kill him, but a witch of any power level could attack you when you least expected it, and you'd be dead. And a bullet is as deadly as a spell. He doesn't follow the rules, Lily. I'd just as soon as you didn't poke the bear with this one. Okay?"

"But can't we swear Chad to secrecy?"

Will and James looked at each other before Will said, "Possibly, but he's a fool, and he'd be the last person to agree to something like that, especially when it's us asking."

"Yes, he seems to take your group as a personal affront, especially Angelica."

"You're not wrong, Mum, but it's a conversation for another day." James looked at me again. "Please just drop it, Lily."

I stared at him. Could I give it up? What if Angelica didn't relent? What if our search of the records didn't turn up anything and the guard was our only lead? I opened my mouth, but I couldn't promise.

James frowned. His voice had a warning tone. "Don't. Okay, just don't. Haven't we been through enough? Hasn't Mum been through enough?"

I swallowed. I couldn't say: no, she hasn't been through enough. Let me get myself killed so she could suffer some more. And he knew it. "But what about Liv and her family? Her demise is just about guaranteed in the short term. Mine is a maybe, and who knows when? I'd be prepared to endure being locked up at home and only going out with protection again."

Will shook his head, disappointment on his face. "And you're assuming we have the resources to do that? What about when your friends can't come and help or can't tag along just so you can go shopping or for a coffee? It's not practical. And what's the alternative? We hunt the guy down and murder him? There's no way we can do that, so then we play another stressful, impractical waiting game. If you care about any of us, you'll leave it alone." He grabbed my hand and squeezed it gently. "I know you're worried about Liv, but there are other ways to solve this."

I made a fist with my other hand and dug my fingernails into my palm. So. Frustrating. "What if we're not quick enough? And why isn't anyone pushing Angelica this hard for her answer?"

Mum stood. "I'll go and talk to her, see if I can get her to see reason."

Footsteps came from the hall. Angelica entered. "Get who to see reason?"

Mum gave her a gentle smile. "You, of course."

Angelica smiled. "I'm afraid you'd be wasting your time."

"Why?" I asked. "Why can't you just give us the information?"

Angelica raised her brow. "I'm going to. I just spoke to my brother and his wife, and they're okay with me giving you what you need."

"Oh. Okay. Thank you." I should've felt relief, but my insides were still wound tight. I doubted the worry would leave until we had Liv here, safe and sound.

Angelica's magic tickled my scalp, and a manila folder appeared in her hand. "Let's sit now, shall we, and I'll fill you all in." I sat in between James and Will on one Chesterfield, and Angelica sat next to Mum on the other. Angelica magicked herself a cup of tea, then started without opening the folder. "Okay, so Beren was adopted when he was two weeks old. His parents were both witches and both killed in a car accident. The closest living relatives were Beren's grandparents on both sides—a grandfather on one side and a grandmother on the other. Neither of them felt capable of taking him in. At the time of his adoption, we had no idea he was a twin."

I blinked. "That's horrible. Why wouldn't they try and adopt them out together?"

Angelica shook her head. "I have no idea, and at the moment, that conjecture isn't going to help us, so it doesn't matter. What I want to find out is who the twin went to, obviously. I've looked up details on the grandparents. The grandmother is still alive, but the grandfather's dead. So I'm going to go and speak with the grandmother."

"That makes sense," said James. "Do you have a current address?"

"Yes. Unfortunately, it's a nursing home, so I have no idea what kind of mental state she's in."

I shuddered, remembering the time Angelica and Beren were almost killed because of an investigation into the Catherine Laboure care home for witches. Will's poor grandmother had been murdered. Yet again, I had to ask why there were so many horrible people in the world. Another reminder why we needed the PIB at full force. I sighed. One thing at a time.

"Can you go today?" James's voice sounded less down than before. This was a huge development.

"Yes. I'm going when we've finished here." She looked at me. "I'd like you to come with me, Lily, just in case we need any photographic evidence of Beren's twin visiting her."

"Okay."

Angelica switched her gaze to my brother. "Can you get Millicent on this ASAP? I don't think the grandmother adopted the twin, but either way, I'm hoping she can solve this puzzle for me without needing to research too much, but just in case, I want our bases covered." She pulled a piece of paper from her folder. "These are the details I have on the grandmother, where she lived when Beren was adopted, her date of birth, Beren's biological parents' dates of birth, and their address when they died. The other information is the witch agency who handled the adoption. So we have a lot to go on if this visit doesn't help. To speed things along, I'd rather double up on research." She pulled another piece of paper from the folder and handed it to James. "This is the address of the care home, just in case." I looked at Angelica. Just in case what? Did she expect something to happen while we were there? Surely not?

James pulled out his phone. "I'm going to call Millicent now. I do want to chase up that security guard. He's the last one who's had contact with the guy, but I'll wait until you can pinpoint where Beren's brother is. We don't want to tip him off."

"Good idea," said Angelica. "The less warning he has, the better. If he knows we're coming, it will put Liv in more immediate danger. If we can't find him where he's supposed to be, you and Will can pay that guard a visit."

James gave her a nod and dialled Millicent. Angelica stood and said bye to my mother. Will put his arms around me and gave me a hug. "It'll all work out. Have faith."

"When you don't have facts, have faith?"

"I don't know about that, Miss Cynical. We have some facts, and we'll get the others. And the future isn't a fact yet, and we can never have that."

I glanced at my mother. If she would let me help her, maybe I could give her magic to use, and she could look into the future, give us an idea of what to expect, maybe more clues, but after our recent argument, there was no way I was going to mount that horse. "Yeah, well, at least we have something." I kissed his cheek and stood. "Let's get this show on the road. Do you have the coordinates?"

Angelica stood. "Of course, dear." She sent them to me mind to mind, and I walked to the middle of the living room, made my doorway, and stuck the coordinates on it. Now it was just a matter of stepping through.

If only everything was that easy.

CHAPTER 8

Getting access to Mrs Caddington had been easy. Angelica pretended to be a friend of her late daughter's who had supposedly grown up with her. The plump, young nurse at the front desk had been very accommodating. "It's not often she gets any visitors. Just mind yourselves, though. She's blind, so make sure you tell her who you are when you're at the door." She'd smiled and pointed us in the direction of her room. A pang of sadness resounded within me. So many old people, forgotten and unloved. Out of sight, out of mind. There was no way I'd ever do that to my mother. If, God forbid, it ever came to that, I would visit her all the time, make sure she knew she was loved, and I had no doubt that James and Millicent would come and bring Annabelle.

The hallway was thick with the same disinfectant-over-layed-with-poo smell that all nursing homes seemed to have. The door was open, but Angelica knocked anyway. A frail voice came from the woman wearing a pink nightgown and lying under white covers. "Hello. Who's there?"

"Mrs Caddington, my name is Angelica DuPree, and I'm here with my niece, Lily." I was her niece now, was I? I supposed she'd been as good as an aunt to me all this time, and she felt like family. Now I just had to pretend Beren was my brother, and we were sweet.

"Hi," I said, thinking Mrs Caddington might like a verbal confirmation.

Angelica continued, "You don't know us, but we'd like to come and speak with you, if that's okay. It's about your grandsons."

The old woman stilled for a few seconds too long, and I was about to check she was still breathing, when she put a hand to her mouth. Her half-closed eyes teared up. After a moment, she moved her hand to her chest. "You adopted one of the boys? I remember now. Please come in." At least she sounded with it, and she hadn't asked us to leave. So far, so good.

"Thank you." Angelica entered and pulled one of the two chairs close to the bed. I grabbed the other and sat next to her. Was Angelica going to correct her or just run with that little white lie?

Mrs Caddington cleared her throat. "I'm not sure I can help you—it was so long ago. What did you want to know?"

"When we adopted Beren, we didn't realise there was a twin. We would've taken both of them."

"How did you find out? We didn't tell anyone, not even the adoption agency."

"My son, Beren, is sitting in jail for a crime he didn't commit, and his girlfriend has been kidnapped by his looka-like. I work for the PIB, and we're investigating. It didn't take long to find their birth certificates." Had she given too much information? One boy was suffering, but would she want to turn in the other one? "I'm sorry to just dump this news on you."

"Oh, my Lord. I—I'm okay, and I am sorry." Mrs Caddington gripped the covers with her gnarled hand.

"Of course, you can see this is time sensitive, which is why we're speaking to you first. Can you tell us who adopted the other boy?"

I shuffled to the edge of my seat, crossed my fingers on both hands, and leaned forward. *Please tell us. Please tell us.*

The old lady blindly stared forward, and her heavy sigh settled over me. It was a sigh of regret, longing, a life that couldn't be. "I tried. I knew there was no way I could bring up both of them. My husband died young, and I never wanted to remarry. I brought up my daughter by myself, and I was too tired to do it with twins, but maybe, I thought, I could do it with one. But it was no use. When the baby was nine months old, I decided he would have a better life with someone who had more money and energy than me." She shut her eyes. "Sometimes love isn't enough. I often wish...."

Angelica, not normally known for her comforting ways, placed a hand on the old lady's that was twisted in the covers. "Life does not often go how we plan or wish it would. If you have any guilt, let it go. You did your best, and no one can ask for more."

"Daniel could. I failed him; I failed my daughter." Her face collapsed in sorrow for a moment. "What about your boy? Before he was arrested, how was his life? Was he happy, healthy?"

Angelica smiled, even though the old woman couldn't see, but the joy came through in her voice. "Yes, very happy. He's a beautiful boy—kind, gentle, a man of principles and action. He has a girlfriend, and they love each other very much. He's good at his job and has many friends, a loving relationship with… his father and me." I blinked back tears. This old lady loved those boys, but she hadn't been able to meet the challenges of raising them. Beren's life had been full of love, and Mrs Caddington had missed out. How often had she thought of them, wondered where they were and how they were getting on? I couldn't imagine the heartbreak of losing her only child and then her grandchildren.

Mrs Caddington's lips curved in a small smile. "Would you please tell him that I always think of him? If only I could see, I'd ask for a picture." Oh my God, if my heart could've broken in two, it would have. My nose tingled uncomfortably as tears threatened.

Angelica squeezed her hand. "He's about six foot two, fair hair, green eyes, beautiful face. He has a joyous smile, and, if I'm not mistaken, he has your chin and cheekbones." Even Angelica teared up at this point. She never did that, but this was her nephew we were talking about. I took my phone out of my pocket and took a photo of the moment. Oh. I frowned. I made the effort to block my magic; then I took another picture. That would be the one Angelica could remember her by, and the one Beren could see. But now we had another reason to get him out of jail ASAP.

"If we can get him out of jail soon, we'll bring him to visit."

Angelica's head whipped around to look at me. Annoyance flashed briefly before she schooled her features. Oh, crap, what had I done wrong?

Angelica looked back at Mrs Caddington. "We're hoping

we can get him out soon, but only if we can find his brother, so I'm afraid it's bittersweet."

The old lady licked her lips. "What did Daniel do that placed your boy in jail?"

Angelica paused, probably weighing up how much to tell her. I mean, she loved the twins, and she already felt guilty for abandoning them to other families. How would the truth affect her? But if Angelica watered it down, would she still be willing to give us the information? "It's a serious matter. He ran someone over, killing them. He's also, as I mentioned before, kidnapped Beren's girlfriend."

The wrinkles on Mrs Caddington's forehead deepened and multiplied. She shut her eyes. Finally, she opened them again and turned her head towards Angelica, her unseeing eyes at Angelica's chest level. "I'm so sorry. This is my fault. I should've kept him or picked a different family. How did I get it so wrong?"

Angelica shook her head. "This is not your fault. Unless your special talent is seeing the future, you made a choice back then based on the information you had. But you do have the power to make something right. Please tell me who adopted Daniel."

"Peter and Sonja Farmer from Assington. They were actual farmers, too, which I thought was amusing at the time. They promised to keep his name, so he would be Daniel John Farmer." She pressed her pale lips together. "What did they do to my grandson?" The Farmer thing was what had amused her? What about Assington? What was it with place names in the UK? There were so many ridiculous ones. On a drive one day, Will took me to Burnt Bottom. If I hadn't seen it with my own eyes, I wouldn't have believed it. If I lived there, I'd probably move just so I didn't have to tell people I was from Burnt

Bottom. Had the people naming these towns been drunk? I could imagine the planning meeting. After a few beers, they all wrote down the silliest names they could think of and put them into a hat, then drew one out. Much laughter probably ensued, and then the town was named. Lucky town.

"I have no idea, maybe nothing, but whatever happened, we will get to the bottom of it. I promise." I stifled a snort at Angelica's mention of bottom. This was neither the time nor the place. *Bum*mer.

"So, will you bring Beren to see me when you can?" She'd opened her eyes wider, and the hope radiating from her saddened me. From what my camera had shown me, she didn't have long left… maybe a day, maybe a week. Could we free Beren in time? But would he even want to come? Oh, was that why Angelica had given me a dirty look? I'd just assumed he'd want to meet his maternal grandmother. *Stupid, Lily*.

"I will, dear. Don't you worry. And your information has been a big help. We appreciate it. I'll be sure to tell Beren what you've done for him."

"I'm just sorry I couldn't do more. And please tell him I love him. I don't know if you can, but when you catch up with Daniel, please tell him I'm sorry, and that I love him too."

Angelica's jaw bunched as she jammed her teeth together. I couldn't see that going down well. For Angelica to comfort a murderer when she just wanted to throw him in jail… well, it might not happen the way Mrs Caddington wanted, but at least she would never know. "Of course I will."

Mrs Caddington smiled. "Thank you for making an old woman happy. I look forward to seeing you again, and hopefully Beren."

Angelica smiled. "Of course." She stood and carefully

placed the old lady's hand on her stomach. "Thank you again, and we'll see you soon. It was lovely to meet you."

"It was lovely to meet you too. Goodbye."

"Bye," I said as I stood. I was first out of the door. Angelica caught up to me and matched my stride as we made our way to the exit room. Nursing homes were generally magic-free so the demented residents didn't accidentally do anything untoward. They also didn't want their residents to disappear. A select few workers could use magic to clean rooms and change beds, but that was it. My talent had still worked because it was a talent, and it only used a fraction of my own magic. But if I'd tried to draw power from the river, it would've failed.

We got the door code for the exit room from the woman at the front desk and entered. "I'll see you back at my place. I'll call James and tell him what we've discovered. Can you call Imani and ask her to come back to mine for a meeting?"

"Can do. I'll see you there soon." I made my doorway and stepped through to Angelica's reception room. After greeting an excited Ted, and Abby, who was civil but totally unexcited in true cat fashion, I made my way to the living room and sat on one of the Chesterfields.

Ted sat at my feet and looked up. *I'm so happy you're here*! His mind voice was joyful and goofy, just like I thought it would be.

I grinned. "I'm happy you're happy." I stroked his head and back. "You're such a cutie." His tongue lolled out, and it looked as if he was smiling. Abby jumped up on the couch, sat next to me on her haunches, then leaned against me and rubbed her head on my arm. "Are you trying to steal attention from Ted?"

Me? Never! I don't need to steal anything. Everybody loves me.

I laughed. "Yes, of course they do." I patted her. "And why wouldn't they?" Did cats understand sarcasm?

Indeed.

Oh, crap, I was supposed to call Imani. "You guys are distracting me." I pulled out my phone and called her. "Hey, meeting at A's as soon as you can get here."

"Okay, cool. See you in ten."

Angelica entered the room and sat on the Chesterfield opposite me. "Will and James will be here soon. Did you get hold of Imani?"

"Yep. She'll be here in ten."

"Good." Her gaze went from poker-faced to serious. "You shouldn't have promised that woman Beren would come and see her."

My cheeks burned. "I know. I'm sorry. Not that this makes much difference, but here." I brought up the photo of Angelica and Mrs Caddington that I'd taken before blocking my magic, and I handed the phone to Angelica.

She stared at the photo. "Oh, I see." She handed the phone back. "So she could die today or tomorrow?"

"Or next week, but her time is close. I would think that Beren should at least be given the choice of meeting her. Maybe he won't want to, but does it hurt to ask?"

"It won't hurt Beren, but it might hurt my brother if he says yes."

"But how? It's not like Beren's saying his parents weren't great or that he wishes he had his birth family. It's part of his history, like it or not. And that woman's had her heart broken terribly by how her life panned out. She lost her only child, and then the other two people who were her only link to her daughter."

Angelica smoothed a hand over her perfect bun. "True,

but it's not Beren's responsibility to make her feel better. Life is sometimes a tragedy, and it's not any particular person's fault. This is one of those situations."

If you say so. I wasn't going to argue with her, but I could still think what I wanted. "Are you going to tell him?"

"I don't know yet." She lifted her gaze from my face to over my head. "Hello, Agent Jawara. Come and sit."

End. Of. Conversation. Fine. I smiled up at Imani before she sat next to Angelica. "Hello. How was work this morning?"

She rolled her eyes, then sat. "Chad's called me five times today to check up on what I was doing, and I've been at work, for what—an hour? He even asked me what Angelica and you were doing today." She smirked. "You've really got him in a tizz."

"Seems I haven't lost my mad skillz, and, yes, I said 'skillz.'"

Imani chuckled. Angelica's expression was thoughtful. "Interesting. He must be under pressure from his superiors." Her wicked grin made me smile. "I hope he's squirming. When we're ready, we'll take advantage of his failed spell, and we'll get some information from him."

"I enjoy a good table turn." I grinned.

"Me too." Imani's magic prickled my scalp, and a cup of tea appeared on the table. "I hope you lot don't mind, but this is the first break I've had this morning."

Angelica waved a casual hand. "Not in the least. Please, enjoy your tea. Would you like a biscuit or two to go with it?"

"Ooh, yes, thanks."

Angelica magicked a plate of biscuits onto the table. Yum, shortbread with vanilla icing-type cream in the middle. There was no way I was letting this opportunity slip through my fingers, so I magicked a cappuccino to myself, picked up a biscuit, and dunked it in. "Oh, wow. Yum!" I mumbled through a full mouth.

Angelica raised a brow. "Manners, please."

I kept my mouth closed. "Mmm m m mmhmm."

She shook her head and rolled her eyes. "Some days, dear, I don't know whether to cry or scream."

I swallowed the last of the biscuit. "Why not do both?"

"*Meow, rrrrrow.*"

"See, Abby agrees with me." I smiled. It was nice to get support from the cat when I couldn't get it from my own species.

Imani's mouth dropped open. "You can talk to them now?"

"Yes! Sorry, I forgot to tell everyone. It happened after my meeting with Chad, after I'd filled you all in and you'd left. One minute I couldn't understand them, the next I could."

"Good for you, dear." Angelica gave me a proud smile, and my stomach warmed at her praise. It was nice to get positive feedback for a change. If she were a teacher, and I was an exam, I'd have red lines and writing all over me. I chuckled. "What's so funny?"

"Oh, ah, I was imagining being a test paper with re—"

She held up her hand in a "stop" motion. "No, don't tell me. It's fine."

Imani smirked. "Lily's brain is a disaster area—you never know what you're going to find. I'm kind of happy about mind shields."

I laughed. "Oh, the things I could distract everyone with…."

Angelica gave me a withering look. "Yes. I can imagine." I grinned and took a sip of my coffee.

Footsteps sounded in the hallway, and a door shut. James and Will must be back. I turned my head in time to see them walk in. "Hello." I waved.

James gave a wave, and Will smiled and came and sat next to me. He kissed my cheek. "How's my gorgeous woman?"

"Good thanks. How are you?"

"Meh, could be better."

James sat next to Imani, and she turned to him. "Your sister can converse with the animals now."

He looked at me. "Oh, good for you. Is it as fantastic as you thought it would be?"

"Hmm." I looked down at Abby, who hadn't moved and was now squished between Will and me. "Sometimes, except when *someone* is hungry when she's already been fed."

"*Mrrrreow.*" *Stop lying. You love it when I talk, no matter what I'm saying.*

"That's debatable." I chuckled.

Will smiled. "I'm glad you won't feel left out anymore. I'm also glad I won't have to translate every five seconds."

Angelica clapped her hands. "Let's get started. Liv is waiting for us to save her, and I'd like to do that as soon as possible." I appreciated her confident tone. She turned to look at James. "Did the interviews turn up anything?"

"No. We only got through a quarter of the ones we had left, but so far, no. Not that we expected to find anything. And what did you find out?"

"Beren's birth grandmother confirmed he was a twin. She tried to bring up the other grandson—Daniel—but she wasn't coping, so she adopted him out to a farming couple. Mr and Mrs Farmer. I've already called Millicent. She's finding a last known address. They were living on a property just outside Assington when they adopted Beren's brother."

James shook his head. "You guys have the worst place names."

I smiled. "I know, right? To be fair, there's a Rooty Hill in Sydney." We both snickered.

"Can we stay on point, please?" Ooh, Angelica was getting angry at James as well. This was a nice change. But what did she expect when she was dealing with a couple of Aussies? There was no situation in which we could let that go unremarked…. Okay, so I'd stayed quiet earlier today, but that had taken supreme effort. Twice in one day was impossible.

James cleared his throat and stopped smiling. "Yes, of course. Please… continue."

"Why, *thank you*." Well, that was sarcasm with a capital s.

Voices came from the hallway just outside the door. I turned. My mother and Millicent walked in. "Hey!" I jumped up and ran around so I could give Millicent a hug. I hadn't seen her for a few days.

"Hey, Lily. How are you?"

"Meh, about as good as I can be, considering what's going on."

"Well, I've got the information on Mr and Mrs Farmer." She held up a piece of paper and made her way to the Chesterfield, squeezing in next to James. I sat back next to Will, and Mum sat next to me.

"What did you find out?" asked James.

"About five years after adopting Daniel, Mr Farmer had a tractor accident and lost an arm. He was only leasing the farm at Assington, so they had nothing to sell. They moved to a nearby village where Mrs Farmer found a job at the local butcher while Mr Farmer looked after Daniel and his older sister. A couple of years after that, according to their bank records, they didn't have much left, and then Mrs Farmer lost her job." Wow, the PIB really could deep dive into people's affairs. The government were total stalkers. Creepy. "After that, they moved to Huddersfield because Mrs Farmer's brother and his family lived there. They rented there until about a year ago when Mrs Farmer died of cancer. Mr Farmer killed himself. From what I can gather, Daniel was still living with them at the time. His last known job was in a factory in the area. It's since closed down."

"Oh, crap. That's horrible. How can so much bad stuff happen to one family?" I frowned. As evil as he'd been lately, the road that got him there was paved with heartache, poverty, and the worst luck ever. It was so depressing that people's lives could go to hell through no fault of their own. That poor family.

"Did you find a current address for him?" Angelica asked.

"The same home he shared with his parents. It's a council terrace."

James and Angelica shared a knowing look. The next step must be to visit that terrace.

I put my hand up. "I have a quick question."

Angelica turned her attention to me. "Yes, dear?"

"His parents were witches, weren't they?"

"Yes."

"So why was life so hard? Surely they could've used their magic in some way to improve their skills or whatever. I mean, I know we can't use it out in the open, in an obvious way, but there must be ways to use it subtly to enhance your abilities with things like carpentry or accounting or even farming. I mean, I don't know, but I just never imagined that witches would be that badly off."

Angelica nodded slowly. "You make a good point, dear. They might all have been weak in the power."

My mother furrowed her brow. "Assington. Isn't there a commune of Renounced? I'm sure we had a case there years ago." She looked at Angelica. "Do you remember that rape and murder case with Evie Bell?"

Recognition registered on Angelica's face. "That's right! There were quite a few of them, somewhere between sixty-five and seventy-five of them."

I took in a shuddering breath. Now that I'd become used to my powers, I couldn't think of anything worse than losing them, and I'd certainly never give them up unless I had an incredibly good reason, like life and death. I needed to be careful what I said, though, because I didn't want to offend my mother. "Renounced? Do they swear not to use their power, or do they burn out on purpose and cut themselves off forever?"

Angelica's expression was grave. "Some do one. Some do the other." Her mouth twisted, and anger flashed in her eyes. "Some cut their children off, severing their ability forever."

Will shook his head. "Deplorable and horrific. Why don't we do more to stop it?"

Angelica raised a brow, giving him a "do you really have to ask" look. "Underfunding, dear, and it's hard to even know about unless someone comes forward to complain."

"From what I've seen, he has his power." In my photo, he'd come through Liv's reception-room door.

"Like I said, dear, we don't have time to discuss this. We'll act as if he has full use of his powers when we pay him a visit."

James leaned forward. "So, when do we go?"

Angelica stood. "Now is as good a time as any. The sooner we find Liv, the better, obviously. And not a word to Chad. We'll follow normal protocol until we have this guy in jail and the evidence gathered. He won't know if no one tells him. It's not like he ever visits the cells."

Imani tilted her head to the side. "He does have a couple of brown-noses who report back to him though, and I haven't figured out who they are."

Will chuckled. "One of them is Agent Brown, funnily enough."

"Which Agent Brown?" James asked. "There are three."

"The short one who never smiles and always says 'well, if you don't say' when someone explains something to him." Will rolled his eyes.

I laughed. "Hmm, that would get old fast. I've managed to avoid him so far. He sounds like another idiot and a perfect ally for our unesteemed ruler."

Angelica looked at Imani. "I think you should accompany Will for this. I want someone fairly impartial as a witness, if nothing else. And, yes, Will is one of Beren's closest friends, but he's imposing, and I think we need that. I don't want to be there in case I'm accused of anything later. Plus, if Daniel has researched Beren's life, family, and friends, he'll know who I am, and it might aggravate him further. I want this to go as smoothly as possible."

James pressed his lips together. "I'd like to be there."

Angelica shook her head. "I don't think it's a good idea. We can afford to lose Will… if Chad gets wind of this and decides to fire someone for disobeying direct orders, but you're in a higher position, and we need the information you're privy to."

Will raised one brow. "You'd throw me to the wolves?"

Angelica's face was as calm as if she were gazing over a sandy beach to the waves beyond. "Yes, dear. If James is there, he has the ability to talk Chad into rehiring you. Don't worry. We have you covered."

He raised the other eyebrow to match the first and gave

her a sceptical look. "If you say so." He stood and addressed Imani. "Okay, Jawara, let's go." He turned to Millicent. "Can I grab the address?" She handed him the piece of paper. "It's half a mile from a landing point. Good." He moved to the middle of the room and looked at Angelica. "I'll call you as soon as we have something." She gave a nod. Will turned to Imani, who had joined him in the middle of the room. "Here are the coordinates." His magic prickled my scalp. I supposed he couldn't make the doorway for both of them because Imani could do without walking into a men's toilet.

They made their doorways and stepped through. I bit my fingernail. My mother frowned. "Lily, stop that!" I took my finger out of my mouth and pouted. "That's better." My leg started jiggling up and down. If she told me to stop that, too, she would be sorely disappointed. Waiting wasn't my strong point, and they were going into a dangerous situation. The guy wasn't shy about killing people, and if he knew Will was one of B's best friends, he'd be in the firing line for sure.

Millicent stood. "Sorry to love you and leave you, but I have work to do. Let me know what happens."

James stood and gave her a quick kiss. "Will do. And thanks for doing that so quickly."

She smiled. "My pleasure." She moved to the middle of the room, made her doorway, and left.

"What now?" I asked.

James sat back down. "Once we have Daniel in custody, we can pick up the guard—we'll need him as a witness."

"Why don't you do it simultaneously?" Honestly, they should just get it over and done with in one go.

"Because if Daniel's not at home and he finds out we took his accomplice, he'll know we're onto him, and he might go underground for a while or do something awful to Liv in retaliation. There are some things that are just as horrible as death. If we can't find Daniel, we'll grab the guard as a last resort."

My heart missed a beat, then thudded heavily. "Right." The last thing I wanted was to make things worse. So waiting it was.

Abby tapped my lap with her paw, then stepped onto it, spun around to get comfortable, and lay down. "*Meeeeowww.*" *Everything will be fine. I love you.*

I stroked my hand along her back. "Thank you. I love you too."

Mum smiled. "Aw, look at you, conversing with the animals. Does that mean we'll be seeing even more squirrels around here?"

"Please, no." Angelica gave my mother a horrified look. "We have enough of those filthy vermin here as it is."

"You'll change your tune when the squirrels save the day."

James chuckled. "You haven't given up that squirrel-army idea yet?"

"Never! It's just on hold." I grinned. "Now that I can actually communicate with them, maybe I can move things along." Hmm, this could be interesting. "Other government agencies have animals helping. Why not the PIB?"

Angelica's eyes widened. "God forbid, dear. The day I need a tree rat to help me do my job is the day I quit."

"We'll see. Also, Chad is running things, and he has less intelligence than a squirrel." I waggled my brows. At least they were playing along with the banter. It was stressful for everyone, the waiting. We all needed a distraction.

Angelica smirked. Score! It wasn't often she was that amused. "True. I may have to rethink my boundaries."

After ten minutes, even the chatter had stopped. We sat in silence, in company with our own thoughts.

Angelica's phone rang, and I jumped, my heart racing. Abby gave me a disgusted look, then settled again. "Will. What have you got for me?" Angelica listened for a minute, her forehead wrinkling. "Okay. I'll get Millicent to look into it. See you soon. Bye." She hung up and placed her phone on the low table between the Chesterfields. "He moved out a week ago. New tenants are in there, non-witches, and they don't know where he went."

James hit his thigh with his fist. "Damn it!"

Angelica sighed. "I know. It's disappointing. Can you call Millicent and ask her to see if he applied for council housing anywhere else? Once we cover that ground, if we have no luck, we'll pay that guard a visit."

Gah, this wasn't good. He could be anywhere. My shoulders slumped, and I sank back into the couch.

James slid his phone out of his pocket and made the call. Soon after he was done, Will and Imani walked in. They filled us in on what happened—which wasn't much except to find out he'd moved away.

Thankfully, we didn't have long before Millicent called back. James grunted a couple of times as he listened. "Yeah, thanks. Bye." He looked at Angelica. "He hasn't applied for council housing. We've hit a dead end."

Will rubbed his forehead. "Not good."

James looked at Will. "No." He started tapping his thigh with one finger, then he drew in a deep breath and sighed. He shifted his gaze to Angelica. "Will, Imani, Lily, and I will handle this one. We'll grab Chris, the guard, and I'll get Lily to take some photos so we can see whether he met with Daniel there or not. If we can get evidence, at least we can satisfy ourselves and push him for information."

She nodded, poker face in place. "Okay. That sounds like a plan."

My mother frowned and looked at me before directing her worried eyes to Angelica. "Does Lily really need to be there?"

Angelica held onto her bland expression, but the small jerk of her head back indicated that my mother's question had surprised her. "Yes. You do know she's aided us in multiple investigations? She's survived numerous attacks and saved others and herself. I wouldn't send her if she weren't capable." My eyes widened. A compliment from Angelica was hard-won at the best of times. Pride warmed my stomach that she was sticking up for me to my mother, and the fact that she really thought I was competent when it came to magic and looking after myself.

My mother's lips pinched together. She moved her gaze to James. "If anything happens to her, you'll have to answer to me." Her warning look scanned over Will and Imani.

James stood, went to her, leaned down, and kissed her cheek. "Don't worry, Mum. If anyone needs saving, it probably won't be Lily. But we'll all make sure she comes back in one piece… and alive." His mouth quirked up on one corner, and he winked.

Mum narrowed her eyes. "She'd better. What happened in Venice was too much of a close call for my liking."

I'd stick up for myself, too, but everyone else had done a pretty good job of it. There was nothing more to be said, not that Mum was taking much in anyway. Why would she worry so much about me and not about James? Maybe she still saw me as a child since I was the youngest. I wouldn't hold it against her, but it was as frustrating as holding the door open for a cat who couldn't decide whether they wanted to come inside or not.

I stood, went to my mother, and put a comforting hand on her shoulder. "We'll be back soon, and I promise I'll be super careful." I smiled and went to the middle of the room where Imani had made a portal. I put up my return to sender and stepped through to a concrete-floored toilet cubicle. Ah, public toilets, how I've missed thee... not. I opened the door and hurried out so Imani had room to enter.

Huh? I turned three hundred and sixty degrees. Imani, Will, and James came out of the toilets and joined me. "Correct me if I'm wrong, but isn't this Hyde Park?"

"Apparently, love. Looks like someone gets paid well." She turned to Will and James. What do guards make at the PIB, anyway?"

Will shrugged, but James said, "It's not the best paying job in the world, but it's not the worst. Thirty-five thousand pounds a year, give or take, depending on what shifts they work—night or day, weekends or weekdays. Some are happy with the normal times, and others prefer to earn more and live like a vampire."

I chuckled. "'Live like a vampire.' Why can't you just call them night owls?"

He shrugged. "Meh, that's where my brain went."

"Where to?" Will asked.

James pulled up a message on his phone. "We're on the wrong side of the park. It's that way." He gave a nod to the north west. "Come on."

We traversed the park and exited on Bayswater Road and turned left. A little way along the busy road, we crossed and walked along a quieter street—Queensborough Terrace. The buildings were gorgeous and stately. A line of yellowy-cream, white, and brown six-storey terraces sat imposingly along the street all the way along. James stopped at one of the buildings.

"This is it. He rents an apartment in here." He stepped under the portico. His magic tickled my scalp. *Click.* He pushed the door open, and we followed him into the foyer, which smelled of disinfectant and oldness, kind of comforting, really. I could imagine the lighting at night, which would glow yellow and inviting. What a lovely place to come home to. Maybe one day....

A wall-mounted board with the unit numbers and the floors they were on told us we needed level two. James looked at Imani and me. "Will and I will take the stairs. You two take the lift. That way, we won't miss him if he happens to be leaving by foot for any reason."

Imani gave a nod, and I pressed the button to call the lift. The door opened immediately. We got in, and I pressed Two. The guys must've run because we only just beat them to the hallway. James whispered, "It's flat two C." He led the way to the door and pulled out his gun—normal police didn't have them over here, but special agents used whatever they needed. Will, Imani, and I fanned out behind James, ready with our magic. James knocked, and I held my breath, listening for telltale footsteps of someone approaching the door.

Nothing.

James looked at Will and gave a thumbs up. He turned back around, and his magic tingled my scalp. He stepped back a pace and kicked the door open. It slammed against the inside wall. The three of them rushed in. I hung back for a moment —I wasn't an agent, and I was liable to get in the way.

A foul odour whooshed out of the apartment. I gagged and choked. What the hell?

Cries of "Clear! Clear!" came from James.

Will's voice. "I've got something here. Damn it!"

I magicked a hand towel to myself from our bathroom and put it over my face. What died in there?

When I entered and found everyone in the kitchen, my question was answered. *Oh, crap.* Chris's body, well, I had to assume it was *his* body, lay on the floor on his back. Blood had crusted a track from both of his ears, down his neck, and onto the floor. There was some mushy-looking stuff on the floor next to his head. I did not want to guess what it was, so I turned, walked back into the living area, and threw open a window. Sticking my head and shoulders out, I grabbed the sill and inhaled the slightly fumy but much sweeter outside air.

There went our witness. Crap.

A woman in a green, sleeveless dress with a flowy knee-length skirt crossed the road, alongside a golden retriever on a lead. Where were they going? Were they having a nice day? Had she ever seen a dead body? Had she ever been in jail? I wasn't going to make the mistake of wishing I was somebody else—we all had our dramas to struggle through—but maybe for a tiny moment, I wanted to be a carefree woman walking her dog on a summery, sunny day, with nothing on my mind but what I might cook for dinner that night.

"Lily." Imani stood behind me.

I took my last breath of "fresh" air, slid the top half of my back into the room, and turned. "You need photos?"

"You know it."

I sighed and pulled my phone out of my back pocket. "I don't suppose you can get rid of that body in there first?"

"No. We need the crime-scene techs to comb over it first."

"Yeah, yeah, fine. Do you at least have some of that stuff people put under their noses?"

She chuckled. "We actually use these." Her magic tingled my scalp, and two small earplug-looking-things appeared in her palm. "They're magicked to inhibit odours getting inside them. Just stick them up your nostrils."

I side-eyed them. "I hope they're new, like, never been used?"

"Of course! Since when would I give you used nostril plugs? You must think I'm a grub."

I folded my arms. "Ah, no, but the PIB are cost-cutting on every level, so…." I raised a brow, as if that proved my point.

She rolled her eyes and pried one hand from my arm fold and shoved them into my palm. "Stick 'em in, and get to work." She turned and went back into the kitchen.

"No one's ever said that to me before. I'm not sure if I feel violated or not," I called out as I shoved them up my nose. I unlocked my phone and called up the camera ap. Time to pull up the big-girl pants and do this.

When I reached the door, Will looked at me. "Don't come in here. Just take the pics from there."

"Okay." His shoes were encased in plastic cover things, so were Imani's and James's, and their magic buzzed around my head like a frenzy of prickly butterflies. They must be gathering evidence the witch way. Well, I couldn't say I was upset at not getting too close to the stinking body. I drew my magic. "Show me who killed Chris."

Daylight shone through the window, so it must've been this morning, after he'd dropped the letter to Beren. His back was to… Ber— no, Daniel. He was making them cups of tea. How civil, and how sad. Had they been friends before this, or was it just a job opportunity? Daniel supposedly had no money, but there was a large envelope on the table with pounds spilling out of it. Had Daniel lived a double life while he'd been with his parents? Maybe he had income or a high-paying job we didn't know about? Wanna-be-Beren held a mallet. He was in full swing, the weighty chunk of metal at the end of the handle an inch from Daniel's head.

Right. *Click.* This was probably all they needed to see. "Here." I handed the phone to Will, who was closest. He took it.

"Oh. Not very subtle."

"Very funny." How could he be making jokes? Maybe when you'd seen so much gory stuff, you had to get through it somehow, and this broke the tension.

Imani took the phone and chuckled. "Ha ha, nice sledge-hammer reference."

I shook my head. "Bloody gruesome lot, you are."

James grabbed the phone and looked at the pic. "Well, when you're knee-deep in this stuff all the time, you have to build a shell, or you'd never get through it." He handed the phone back down the line, but his gaze when it landed on me contained no light-heartedness. "Don't worry, Lily. We have nightmares just like you do."

I frowned. "I know. Sorry. It's just…."

"Don't worry about it. You don't have to understand." He gave me a sad smile. "We don't need you anymore. If you want to go, feel free."

I gave him a grateful smile. "Thank you. Is there anything you want me to do?"

"Just show the picture to Angelica and explain what we found." At least that was something I couldn't stuff up.

"Okay, consider it done. If you need anything else, call me. Oh, do you want me to ask Millicent to see if she can find his bank account? That looked like a lot of cash on the counter, and it's not here now."

"Good idea. Yes, please. Nice pick up."

"Thanks, bro." I gave them a wave. "Good luck." I

turned and made my doorway. As soon as I let myself in from the reception room to the hallway, I called out, "Hello!"

The only answers I got were a meow and a bark. Abby and Ted came and greeted me. "Hey, you two. Do you know where Mum and Angelica went?"

"Meow. Rrrrow." Angelica said something about headquarters before they left through her portal.

"Thanks." I unlocked my phone and called Millicent. "Hey."

"Hi, Lily. What's up?"

I explained the situation. "So, do you think you could check out his bank details? It might help pinpoint where he's living if we can find a branch, or even where he took the money out, and where it came from in the first place."

"I certainly can."

"Can you do me another favour?"

"Of course. What is it?"

"I need to have a shower. I'm pretty sure I brought the stink of the dead back here." I sniffed my T-shirt and hair. Yep. Gross. The stench clung. I shuddered. "Anyway, I need you to tell Angelica what I just told you. Also, James didn't say, but I'm pretty sure Chad's going to have to find out eventually since James is calling in the forensics guys. We have proof of what happened, but they're going to have to piece it together from the evidence."

"Righto. I'll let her know as soon as I get off the phone, and I'll call James with any information I dig up."

"You're a star. Thanks, Mill."

I got off the phone and ran upstairs. The warm shower was the best thing ever, and so was washing my hair and getting into a clean T-shirt and shorts. Sometimes it was the little things in life that pleased me the most. The joy of being comfortable and clean could never be underestimated.

My stomach grumbled. Perfect timing. I'd enjoy a quiet lunch, then call James and see how everything was going. Abby met me at the bottom of the stairs. *"Meow?" Can you give a girl some tuna?*

I laughed. "I suppose so." Just as I reached the kitchen door, a knock sounded on the reception-room door. I smiled. It must be Imani or James—neither of them had a key. Looked like I'd have company for lunch—well, other than Abby—and find out the news sooner than expected. I hurried to the door and opened it. "Hey!" Oh. I blinked. That wasn't Imani or James. It was a tall guy with broad shoulders in his twenties. His shoulder-length brown hair was a mass of curls obscuring his eyes, like a dog in dire need of a groom. "Can I help you?"

His hesitant smile finally settled into a straight line. "Um, I'm delivering an invitation."

"Oh? Who's it for?"

"Lily Bianchi. Is she here?"

"That's me." I smiled and held out my hand.

"Ah, good. Here it is then." He pulled an envelope out of the satchel hanging from his shoulder and offered it to me.

I reached out and took it, and he grabbed my wrist. His magic tingled my scalp, and a flash of silver shone in his other hand. He slapped it on my wrist. The bracelet closed and locked. *Click.*

What. The. Hell? I reached for my magic.

Nothing.

Dammit! Nooooooooooo! My heart raced. What was coming next?

He gave me an apologetic smile. "Sorry, but if you read

the invitation, you'll see you're needed at Dan— I mean Beren's wedding to Olivia."

I would've kicked him in the stomach and run, but this new information had me freezing. I swallowed my fear, which landed with a heavy splash in my stomach. "Why would I be needed at their wedding?"

"You're the maid of honour. I'm the best man." He stood up straighter and gave me a genuine smile. I was inclined to think he might not be all there if he was happy about this. He obviously knew Daniel wasn't Beren. Did he know where Olivia had come from, or had Daniel lied to him? But then again, why would he think he needed to stick a magic-blocking bracelet on the maid of honour. That wasn't how this wedding thing normally went. I mean, it was hard work being in the bridal party, what with organising parties and dresses and shoes and keeping the bride calm and happy on her big day, but kidnapping to get one there?

"When is the… wedding?" This was not happening.

"This evening." At least this meant she was still alive. It was as if someone were touching my hip, and I jumped back. My phone floated in the air. Daniel's mate's tongue was poking out of his mouth as he concentrated. The phone shot down the hall, through the kitchen door, and clattered to the floor.

Anger surged through me. "You better not have broken it!"

He cringed. "Sorry. I— I'm not too good at the magic stuff. Come on." He grabbed my arm, his fingers digging in painfully. I wanted to pull against it and escape, but Liv needed me. He turned and dragged me into the reception room. He must be making a doorway. I couldn't see it because my magic was blocked. So frustrating.

He dragged me through it. Adrenaline surged through my blood. Was I making the biggest mistake of my life? I stumbled out the other side into a large reception room with two ratty brown armchairs, a large dead pot plant in between them. As kidnapper guy unlocked the door, I narrowed my eyes. Had I imagined the flash of brown and white at my feet as we went through? *Abby*? No answer. Damn. Not that I wanted her in danger, too, but maybe she could've helped me somehow. As it was, she could tell Will what had happened—which was better than nothing. And boy, was I going to be in massive trouble for being so lax when answering the door. But who would've thought the enemy would want to knock on our door, step into the lion's den, so to speak? Although it was more of an idiot's den when I was home alone… apparently.

Daniel's lackey opened the reception-room door and dragged me through, then closed and locked it. My mouth dropped open. The foyer was not what I'd been expecting after the crappy furniture in the reception room. A crystal chandelier hung from the high ceiling. Black and white tiles lay underfoot, and the front door to the non-witch world was a massive, white-painted timber affair with a fanlight above. Shafts of afternoon sunlight streamed in. It was a home I'd imagine a rich person lived in.

Had they broken into a house where the people were away? Was Liv already here?

The guy, who hadn't let go of my arm, dragged me through into a large formal living room. For a room that could hold at least what Angelica's living room did, it was sparsely furnished. A two-seater brown leather couch sat on the bare timber floor—no rug or carpet. That was it. No ornaments adorned the stone fireplace. No paintings hung on the pristine eggshell-blue walls.

Where was Liv?

I looked up at the stranger's face, considering my options.

He was taller than me by a few inches. His shoulders were broad but not too muscled. I could probably take him if I kicked him in the nuts first, even without my magic. He didn't seem to have a super aggressive nature—he'd apologised for not being good at magic. Mean thugs didn't do that. Not that he wasn't dangerous. He just broke more than one law by cutting me off from my magic and kidnapping me, not to mention colluding with a murderer and kidnapper.

But just say I did fell him and get away; I still had no magic and no idea where Liv was. And if Daniel was standing guard over her, he would have the magic and psycho advantage. He'd already killed once. I didn't want to be next.

Be patient. An opportunity will come. Hmm, it hadn't come for me to save myself and Angelica in Italy. I'd had to rely on the luck that someone else would find me and care enough to do something about it. *Stop thinking unhelpful thoughts, Lily! Okay, brain.*

After that wholly unhelpful conversation with myself, I realised Lackey Guy had taken me into yet another room, which looked to be another sitting room with a view of a massive backyard. An immaculate lawn stretched out from french doors. There didn't seem to be a back fence, just large trees. Damn it! There weren't even any other houses. Screaming in the hope that a neighbour might hear was out. Were we in the middle of a forest?

Lackey Guy stopped, jerking me to a halt. "Ow! Can you be more careful? You're hurting my arm." I would try and be patient in terms of finding Liv, but I couldn't be quiet about everything.

He looked at me through the small gaps in his hair. "Sorry." He wasn't, though, because he didn't loosen his grip. He shouted, "Daniel! We're back! Where are you?" So he wasn't pretending it was Beren anymore? For the second time, it was apparent that he wasn't the sharpest tool in the shed. Hopefully that would work to my advantage soon.

Booted footsteps came from the other living room. Then Ber— ah, Daniel, came through the door. I hated myself for gasping, but… Beren stood there. My gorgeous friend, one of the kindest people I knew.

Only it wasn't.

An evil glint in his eyes overshadowed his wide grin. "Good work, Tom. You've brought the pig to market." He came over and slapped his mate on the back while laughing at his own stupid joke. His voice was lower than Beren's, and he dropped the tees at the end of the words, unlike Beren, who rounded his words and gave a smooth delivery. Beren's accent was the result of a middle- to upper-class life. Just in this, it was apparent how different their experiences had been. Not that poorer families couldn't be loving and kind, their children smart and friendly. He'd missed out on that, though. The whole thing was a tragedy.

And now Liv, Beren, and I had to deal with the consequences.

Daniel stared at me and smirked. "You're a lovely one, then, ain't ya? I bet me brother had a go at you." His knowing —and completely off the mark—laugh drew goosebumps out on my arms. He was gross, and if he tried to touch me, patience be damned. He would regret it.

It was almost impossible to reconcile the fact that it wasn't Beren in front of me. If he wasn't speaking, the anger and ill intent shining from his eyes was the only point of difference between him and his brother. Unnerving. It was hard not to do a double take every five seconds on loop.

"What do you want me to do with her?" Tom asked.

"Put her upstairs with the bride." He grinned. "We'll magic them into some clothes soon. I just wanna make sure everything in the back is ready."

Tom nodded, then dragged me out of a door, down a hallway, and to a staircase. We went to the first floor and then to the end of another corridor. Was I really going to see Liv? What condition was she in? My palms sweated, and I desperately wanted to run. I jerked my head around, but there was nothing to see and nowhere to go. Tom's grip on my arm tightened as he magicked the door open. He shoved me inside, and I flew forward, just getting my feet underneath me in time not to fall on my face. He slammed the door shut, leaving me.

I stood still and lifted my head.

"Lily! I knew you'd come!" Liv jumped off the bed and threw her arms around me.

The familiar burn in my nose and throat ended in tears as I hugged her back. "Oh God, Liv. We've been so worried." I eased back and looked at her. Her face looked good, and she didn't have any obvious injuries.

"Why have you been worried?" She wore a ghost of a smile, and two small divots sat in the space atop her nose, as if she were confused.

"You've been missing. That guy kidnapped you. He killed someone, Liv. We thought he'd hurt you... or worse."

Her forehead wrinkled. "What are you talking about. Are you serious? This is Beren you're talking about. We just took a few days for a romantic getaway, and now we're getting married!"

Crap.

I couldn't even access my magic to see how he'd tampered with her brain. Evil witch. If he'd caused any permanent damage, I'd chop his fingers off, one by one. Argh! I wanted to scream. How could there be so many horrible witches out there? And why did we have the pleasure of meeting every one of them?

I could try and convince her of the truth, but whatever spell Daniel had cast would likely override her desire to believe me. Ah, stuff it. I still had to try. "This isn't Beren. His name is Daniel."

Her lips flattened, pressing together. She took a step back from me and planted her hands on her hips. "Stop being stupid, Lily. I haven't seen you for ages, and I don't want to argue. Please don't joke around like that on my wedding day. Honestly, I know you like to make people laugh, but this is just upsetting me."

I sighed. Sorrow burrowed into every cell, the enormity of what I had to do all too clear. Not only would I have to try and save her by myself with no magic, I'd have to do it against her altered will. Was I going to have to drag her out of here? I glanced around, but there was no phone lying out in the open. "Where's your phone?"

She shrugged. "It ran out of charge."

"But do you know where it is?"

Her face blanked, and she stared at nothing before shaking her head. "Somewhere. But it doesn't matter because Beren's got everything under control. He's been the best. You know he organised the whole wedding?"

I tried to keep the sarcasm out of my voice. "Isn't he so great! What a catch!" I took a deep breath and shut my mouth. Screaming wasn't going to achieve anything but upset Liv, and this wasn't her fault. And who was the idiot witch who'd been kidnapped yet again with no one knowing where the hell I was? I should consider getting a tracking chip put under my skin. I wasn't joking, and if I got out of this alive, everyone else would probably love that idea.

Male cheering, then laughter came from outside. I hurried to the window. This bedroom overlooked the side yard, rather than the rear. There was a timber target set up in the shape of a deer. A knife stuck out of the target's face, and Daniel stood about twenty-five feet from it, another knife poised in his hand. He let fly, and it bounced off the target's stomach and fell to the grass. "Oooh! Bad luck." Tom patted him on the back and handed him another knife. Daniel set himself up and threw again. It thunked cleanly into the deer's chest area.

Liv had come to stand next to me. "It's those agent skills coming through. Isn't he good?" She smiled.

"Hmm, if you say so."

She didn't even respond to my cattiness. The serene look on her face was put there by magic, after all. It was going to take a lot to shift her adoration of Beren's nemesis. Maybe we could attempt an escape while they were occupied? I went to the door and tried the handle. Locked. Of course it was. *Idiot, Lily.*

I turned back to Liv. "What time is the wedding?"

"I don't know. Beren said it will be a romantic evening wedding. He's going to come up and magic on our outfits later. He's having his stag's afternoon."

Oh, so that's what the knife-throwing was about. Part of me wondered if it was also a quiet threat—we have magic *and* knives. Not that he probably thought I was dangerous without my magic. It wasn't like I was a trained agent. Hmm. Daniel had obviously put some kind of mind control on Liv, which meant he'd probably read her mind and knew all about me— what I could and couldn't do. Crap. He was twice the threat, since Liv knew my secrets. Whether he'd choose to use that information and me was another matter. As if things weren't complicated enough. I bit my fingernail.

"Don't do that!" Liv grabbed my hand and gently lowered it. "Today is a happy day. Aren't you happy for me?"

"I'm happy I'm here for you."

Hurt glinted from her eyes. "Don't you like Beren?"

I shook my head. "I love Beren. He's one of my best friends." *But he's not Beren, and we're in so much trouble.*

"Oh, good. It's just... you're acting weird."

I'm acting weird? Okay, so she had an excuse, but it was no less painful for me to live through. My eyes widened. I tried to school my face to neutral. *You can channel an Angelica poker face. Come on.* "Have you and Beren been... um... sleeping together?"

She laughed. "He said he's saving it for the wedding night. He said it would be more special if we stopped for a while before the wedding."

Thank God for that. Otherwise, I didn't think he'd survive Will and James catching up to him. And how would Liv feel when we took his spell away and she knew what had happened? I couldn't let it come to that. I would die first. So I only had until tonight to figure this out. Great. Just great.

As much as I didn't want to upset Liv, I couldn't help nudging her a bit. "So, can we go for a walk or something, check out the property? It looks huge."

She bit her lip. "Oh, um. I don't think Beren thinks it's a good idea."

"Why not?"

Her brows drew down as she thought. After a minute, she said, "It's just not a good idea. There's some wild dogs or something that we need to be careful of."

"But *he's* outside."

"He has those knives to protect himself."

I smiled. "I have my magic." For all she knew, I had it, anyway.

She frowned and stared out the window. "Last time I asked him, he got really mad and said if I didn't just trust him, the wedding was off."

Now wasn't the time to discuss abusive relationships, and the Liv I knew wouldn't put up with that if she were in her right mind. I'd just have to figure out what we would do when the wedding was happening. "So, now what do we do?"

"Wanna play Uno?"

I smiled and ignored the slithery sensation cascading down my spine. "Sounds good." I guessed if we had to wait till later, we might as keep ourselves distracted.

For all I knew, this could be the last fun we ever had together. Better make it awesome.

CHAPTER 9

There was no clock in Olivia's room. The light outside the window had me guessing that it might be some-where around 6:00 p.m. My stomach grumbled. I'd been offered strawberries, but I didn't trust them not to drug me, so I declined. Not that they couldn't spell me to sleep, but they would have to know the spell and be careful to not make it too strong, since I was supposed to be attending a wedding soon. Maybe they'd drug me just enough to stop me thinking straight. Even though the bracelet stopped me accessing my powers, I could stop them reading my mind. It only took a trickle of my life-essence magic, and there was no way I was relinquishing that protection. I just had to hope they didn't threaten to hurt Liv.

The door lock clicked, and the handle turned. The door opened, and Daniel stood there. My heart skipped, then raced. How was he not Beren? The likeness was uncanny, and I didn't think I'd ever get used to it.

Liv jumped off the bed and flew into his arms. "B! Have you brought my dress?"

Daniel flicked his gaze to me, then smirked, pulled Liv into his arms, and pashed her senseless. Hatred roiled in my stomach, and I clenched my fists and my teeth. Magic or no magic, I could still right hook him. Boy, was it an effort not to.

When he was done showing off, he grinned at Liv. "I have your dress."

Her eyes lit up. She clapped her hands. "Show me!"

A white dress appeared in his arms. I wasn't sure if it could be called a gown. The skirt looked short. In fact, there was way less material than there should be. So, we were having a trashy wedding, and why would I think it would be any different for a man who thought women were objects to own or use, and who kidnapped and murdered because he wanted to ruin another man's life?

I threw another piece of wood on the bonfire of rage within me.

He handed the dress to Liv, then looked at me. Another dress appeared in his arms, and a pair of shoes. The dress was black, and there wasn't as much material in that one as I would've liked. At least the weather was warm. What a nightmare it would've been if it was winter. He gave me the dress, the pair of black stilettos, and another smirk. "Get dressed. Can't wait to see you ladies all tarted up." *Yeah, just can't wait.* I rolled my eyes, but he didn't notice because he was busy winking at Liv. Ew. I hoped seeing this guy be horrible didn't make me look at Beren differently. The whole thing was weird and creepy.

Thankfully, he left after that. Yay that we could dress in private. At a pinch, I could use these shoes as a weapon—I'd checked Liv's room out, and there was nothing else I could hurt someone with. The three-inch spiky heel could totally kill someone if you speared them in the eye. At the very least, you could stomp on a foot, impale them, and run… maybe not in the shoes, but if that happened, I'd keep one in my hand, just in case. The only problem was getting Liv to come with me. There was no way I could carry her and move fast enough to outrun a man, and definitely not a man with magic.

I looked at the silver magic-blocking bracelet on my wrist. Should I try and break it? I bit my fingernail and studied the shiny surface. There was not a join to be seen, but magic was involved, so all I had to do was focus my power on it, and the energy would do the rest. Unfortunately, it would take monumental effort, and if it didn't work, I'd be too vulnerable after depleting my internal stores. Maybe I should have a poke around. Just a small one.

"Lily?"

Crap. Liv was talking to me. "Yes?"

"We have to get dressed." She smiled. "You can just magic yours on."

"I can't. Your fiancé put this bracelet on to stop me. He's blocking my magic."

She bit her lip as she looked at the torture jewellery. "Surely not. You're just imagining things." Her gaze moved to mine. "Just get dressed. I don't want to be late."

This is not really Liv. If I didn't remember that, I was liable to scream at her or shake her. When someone you loved's eyes were closed to the truth, it was one of the most infuriating things ever.

As I took my T-shirt and shorts off and slid the dress on, I channelled a miniscule amount of power into the manacle. I shut my eyes for a moment to concentrate. My life force slid around the metal and reached a fine crack that I could sense rather than see. But instead of pushing the crack open, the magic was sucked in and disappeared. Crap.

"Are you tired?"

I opened my eyes. Liv stared at me. Oh God. She was wearing her white dress, but that was the only weddingish thing about it. It finished just above mid-thigh and had a deep V, exposing so much cleavage. If there was one wrong movement, I was going to see one or both nipples. She never ever in a gazillion years would've chosen this dress to marry Beren in. This wasn't her dream wedding. It was Daniel's.

And I'd do whatever I could to ruin it.

But Liv. It was her wedding day, just not the one she was meant to have. Tears seared my eyes, and I was thankful I wasn't wearing make-up. An oversight from Daniel, the overlord. My heart broke for her and Beren. I swallowed my despair because right now, she needed to hear she looked gorgeous. "You look beautiful. Do you have a veil?"

"Um, I'm not sure."

A quick head turn told me all I needed to know. "Well, you don't need one. You're so gorgeous; let everyone see your face." Hmm, *everyone*. There were only four of us attending this wedding, and Liv wasn't going to see herself. Hopefully there wouldn't be any photos. I stared past Liv to the wall. Who was officiating the wedding? Did Daniel know someone capable of carrying it out and keeping quiet?

She tilted her head and gave me a once-over. "You look lovely. I don't think I've ever seen you expose so much cleavage. You should do it more often. I bet Will would love it."

I looked down at said cleavage. It was bursting out all over the place, and even though my skirt was knee-length, the split going all the way from knee to hip ensured there was quite a breeze where there shouldn't be. I had an almost uncontrollable urge to fold my arms over my chest. Walking into a potential battle was the last place I wanted to feel exposed. Unless it worked to my advantage. Distraction was a ploy. Not that they'd definitely be distracted by my body, but I kept in shape. I could try and be sexy, but I'd probably look consti-pated more than anything if I tried to pout and walk with super swaying hips. I had no idea how to be sexy. Lucky for me that Will didn't care. Which reminded me, I hadn't shaved my armpits for a few days. Not that there was a lot of growth, but there was enough that if this was something I'd chosen to wear out, I would've been loath to lift my arms. Maybe I could gross Daniel out instead and shove my hairy armpits into his face. Hmm....

The bedroom door swung open, and I started. But no one was there. Damn, I hated not being able to access my power. I couldn't tell who was channelling magic and when. It was like knowing a spider was in the room but not knowing where it was going to scurry or pounce from.

I put my hand on my tummy and tried to soothe the nausea growing there. If I couldn't think of something soon, this was going to end in massive disaster.

Liv grabbed my hand. "This is it." A bouquet of red roses tied with a white ribbon appeared on the bed. Her mouth fell open. She reached down to pick them up. "They're gorgeous," she breathed.

"Yes, totally." The colour of highly oxygenated blood. If the real Beren had given them to her, I would've said the colour of passion. But here we were.

"I guess it's time to go." She gave me a nervous smile.

I did my best to smile back, but it was probably more like a grimace. Attempting to kill someone with your shoe wasn't a great plan, but it was all I had. Maybe I should just sacrifice myself if it came to that—all or nothing. Try and get the bracelet off because what was the point if I didn't? Was I giving up too easily? Maybe Millicent was finding information right now about where Daniel was. He might have used his or Beren's name to rent or buy this property. After all, he didn't know that we knew who he was. Maybe I'd wait a day or two before I used all my power, just in case. *Patience, Lily.*

"You have to go first. Beren told me last night that there will be rose petals to follow once we reach the top of the stairs." She giggled. "He's so romantic."

"Mmhmm." Goosebumps peppered my arms as I walked, or was that wobbled, through the bedroom door—these shoes were way too perilous. Maybe they'd kill me before I got a chance to poke Daniel's brain via his eye.

As I traversed the corridor, my wide eyes took in as much as possible. If there was anything I could use as a weapon, I'd grab it. Not sure where I could hide it in this skimpy dress, but I'd damn well try.

When I reached the top of the stairs, Liv exited the bedroom. She grinned at me. I gave her a sad smile—it was all I could manage. My nerves were tangled worse than a slinky that had been out of the box for five minutes. And like a mangled slinky, there was no easy way of fixing this.

I gripped the bannister as I descended, following the trail of red rose petals. Breaking my neck falling down the stairs was not the way I wanted to die. And knowing these guys, they'd bury me here somewhere, and no one would ever know what had happened. Such happy thoughts for a wedding day. Gah! *You have to get out of this so you can attend Liv's real wedding one day.* Not that Beren had proposed to her yet, but if we all survived this, he might be tempted.

At the bottom of the stairs, the petals led down the hallway, to the sitting room with the french doors, and out into the backyard. The evening light cast a yellowish luminosity over the border hedges and blue irises that grew in front of them. A line of camellia trees decorated the other side of the garden, pinkish-white leaves soft and magical, making everything so much prettier. I shook my head. This was not the time to get caught up in how alluring and ethereal the garden was, with small bugs flitting this way and that. They almost looked like fairies in the early evening glow. A rustle in the camellias caught my attention. Two squirrels scurried up the trunk and hid in the foliage. So cute, and so clueless as to our predicament.

Daniel stood in the middle of the grassed area, under a white arch, hands clasped one over the other in front of his crotch. Target, anyone? He saw me and smirked. His gaze travelled from my face to my boobs to my legs. A shiver of disgust wracked my body. He'd killed that poor woman as a means to an end. What was he going to do with me when he'd finished with this charade? There was no way he was letting me go.

Tom stood next to Daniel. Both looked dapper in their tuxedos. Oh, how looks could be deceiving. I'd always found Beren's features attractive, and so it was with his brother. Which was more than disconcerting. I had to keep reminding myself that he wasn't Beren. Daniel's evilness more than diminished his attractiveness to zero. I conjured my hatred and held it tight.

Whilst the garden borders to the left and right had hedging and camellias, in the area behind Daniel, where no hint of a fence could be seen, large trees crowded into the distance. Definitely no neighbours there. No one to hear me scream, which, ironically, made me want to scream all the more.

I swallowed the fear inching up my throat.

Behind both men stood a short, slim man in his forties. He wore a navy-blue suit and held a large maroon-covered book in both hands. A celebrant? Witch or human? A human would be easier to control. Daniel could, if he had the skills, mind wipe him when we were done. I'd rather that than he had yet another friend who thought all this was acceptable.

I crossed the lawn and reached the men, then stood to the side. Tom smiled at me. I gave him a dirty look. He had the decency to correct his mistake by losing the smile and looking away. *If I had my magic, I'd set your pants on fire, starting with the crotch.*

I turned towards the french doors. Liv stood in the doorway, the fading rays of sun catching in her dark hair, bringing out rich red glints. Even without make-up, she was stunning, her smooth light-brown skin and defined cheekbones giving her a model look. And because she truly believed she was marrying the man of her dreams, her face radiated joy brighter than the sun.

I promise you I'll fix this, Liv. I'll put you back with the right man if it's the last thing I do.

God, if Beren and everyone knew what was going down right now, they'd probably feel worse than what they already did. Anger, sharp and hot, lanced my stomach, and regret constricted my heart. This was my fault… well, not all of it, but how could I have just opened the door, then let him take me? Was it better I was here without my magic than not here at all? Even if I thought the answer to that was yes, Will, Mum, Angelica, James, Imani… they would all be worried and as mad as a cut snake. Even if I survived this, I was in for some kind of reckoning… again. Boy, was I sick of being in trouble. Maybe I should see if Will wanted to move to Australia.

Nothing ever happened to me when I lived there… except losing my parents, but that happened to them over here, so it didn't count.

Both men watched Liv walk towards us. Daniel licked his lips. His wolfish smile sent my heart racing, and not in a good way. Tonight was the night. I couldn't let it happen. Could. Not.

So, think, dammit.

Rustling came from behind us, and I turned. More squirrels. I couldn't even get excited at how cute they were because I'd left my little army at home, and now I couldn't even talk to animals because my magic was cut off. Grrrr. So other than being cute and furry, they couldn't help me.

But then something caught my gaze. A pair of green eyes peering at me from behind a tree. I quickly turned back to Liv, who had reached us. She smiled up at Daniel. I hid my excitement. Abby *was* here! Clever cat. Even if she'd been able to tell Will what had happened to me, they couldn't have ever found us with that information. Better she was here and could help me. She knew about my squirrel army, and maybe we could get them to help us by attacking Daniel and Tom. But that might lead to squirrel casualties.

Could I do it and live with myself afterwards if some died?

Yes, the human life of someone I loved was more precious to me than one squirrel, but I still didn't want to condemn any of my cute friends to death. Still, I needed to try something. But how would I tell Abby what I wanted? *Think, Lily.*

Liv and Daniel faced each other, and the short guy opened his book. "Ladies and gentlemen, we are gathered here today to celebrate the marriage of Beren DuPree to Olivia Grosvenor." Hmm, I saw no gentlemen. That was an oversight on the celebrant's part.

I put up my hand. The celebrant stopped talking and gave me a "not now" look. I ignored him. Cats had good hearing, but I wanted to be sure, so I spoke loudly. "Can we do this without a squirrel army?"

Liv's head snapped around to stare at me, and annoyance flickered in Daniel's glare. Liv gave me a "what are you doing?" stare. "Lily, I know squirrels are your favourite subject, but now is not the time."

"Sorry, but I just think this wedding would be better with lots of squirrels swarming all over the place. They're good at making a bad situation better."

Her eyes widened. "How is this a bad situation? You haven't been yourself since you got here, and I'm thinking that inviting you was a bad idea."

Daniel patted her arm. "Don't worry, hottie. I'll deal with this." Hottie? Didn't even that bit of information penetrate the depths of her brain to let her know it wasn't Beren? Daniel stepped up to me and loomed. "Just stop. You can see this is what Olivia wants." There was that bloody smirk again. "If you interrupt us again, I'm afraid I'll have to ask you to leave." He cut his finger across his throat in the universal symbol for "you're dead." Olivia didn't see it because his back was to her. I stuck my middle finger up at him to show him how I felt about that. His eyes widened, and a cloud of rage passed across the sun, shadowing his face.

I didn't have any advantages right now, but I could try and psyche him out, put a tiny bit of doubt into his brain. I narrowed my eyes. "You have no idea who you're dealing with. Watch your back, Daniel." I knew he did because he'd probably read Olivia's mind, and this was meant to scare him. I was the person who could break out of magical shackles, and I'd killed more people than he had... at least I thought I had.

Maybe he was a serial killer, and we didn't know. But anyway….

He gritted his teeth and ground out, "Don't call me that, witch. My name is Beren."

"You wish."

The slap came out of nowhere, the crack ringing out over the pathetic excuse for a wedding. Birds flew from branches. My eyes watered from the burning sting, but I refused to put my hand up and soothe it. I raised my chin and stared him down. "Like I said, *Daniel*, you have no idea who you're dealing with. Imagine how your parents would feel, knowing what you're doing now? I heard your dad recently died."

His eyes registered surprise, then rage clouded over them. He lifted a hand, but I refused to cringe away. Olivia stepped next to him and grabbed his forearm. "What are you doing?"

"Your witch of a friend is saying some horrible things to me. I can't believe I welcomed her into our home."

Olivia's face blanked. It was as if she was torn between what old Olivia knew and what brainwashed Olivia believed. Brainwashed Olivia won out. "I'm sorry, sweetie." She looked at me. "I'm sorry, Lily, but you'll have to leave."

"Okay, gladly." I gave Daniel a "sucked in" smile because maybe this was my ticket out of there. Okay, so I didn't really believe that, but a girl could dream, plus, I wasn't about to leave Olivia alone with them.

Daniel gave Tom a nod and put his arms around Liv, moving her away and back to the celebrant. Tom stalked towards me, and I backed up a few steps, the heels of my shoes sinking into the grass, slowing me. He grabbed my arm and dragged me towards the house. Instead of going inside, he kept walking around until we were out the front. I couldn't see Liv anymore. My pulse throbbed in my throat. I had to hope that nothing happened to her while I was gone. Because make no mistake: I was going to return.

I yanked backwards against Tom's hold. "Just stop! I've twisted my ankle." I whimpered. "It hurts." He showed before that he either wasn't 100 per cent smart or 100 per cent cruel; either way, he should stop.

"Oh, okay."

Phew! Now I had to hope that there was a squirrel or two to provide a distraction. Hopefully, Abby had figured out what I wanted. I bent to take off my shoe and rub my ankle. That's when I noticed a lovely blue glazed pot with a small fern in it. The pot was a similar size to a kettlebell—the perfect weight for smashing the back of someone's head.

Things were looking up… well, maybe not for Tom, but they were for me.

I took my shoes off.

"What are you doing?"

"My feet hurt, and so does my ankle. Can you just give me a minute?" I looked up at him, giving the impression I was helpless and not at all about to try and almost kill him.

He looked down at me and said nothing for longer than expected. This must be a really tough decision. *Don't strain any brain cells, mate.* My mouth dropped open. Had I said that? Hmm, no, I didn't think so. Phew.

A cat yowled in the hedges behind Tom. My heart kicked into a frenzied beat. He turned to look, and as soon as he did, I dropped my shoes and picked up the pot plant. As I jumped to my feet, I hefted it over my head, then held my breath as I used every ounce of strength I had to smash it into the back of his skull.

He made a kind of *oof* grunt, which was hard to hear over the thud. My stomach somersaulted at the crunch-crack combination of impact. He fell forward like a toppled tree and crashed face first into the grass. I didn't see any brains, just some blood, so he hopefully wasn't dead. I checked for a pulse —yep, there was one. I also checked his pockets for any kind of key. Not that he'd likely be carrying one for my bracelet, and it might even need a spell to unlock, but I couldn't not check. Not checking would be the second dumbest thing I'd done today.

Nothing. Pfft.

Armed with my shoes, I crept to the front wall of the house at the corner. A rustling came from the hedge, and Abby poked her head out and blinked at me. I smiled and gave her a thumbs up. I whispered as loudly as I dared, hoping she could hear me over the few feet. "Can we get an attack on Daniel's legs, then face?"

She nodded. This had been almost too easy. Surely something was going to go wrong.

Stop it, Lily! Don't sabotage yourself. Yeah, why should I when the universe always managed so well? I calmed my shallow breaths. Being in constant fear for a few hours was hard work, and this was *it*—the moment of success or failure.

I had two problems. Problem one: overcoming Daniel without magic. Almost impossible, but I had to try. Problem two: even if I did manage to knock him out, getting Liv to come with me once that was done was going to be almost as impossible as problem one. I sighed. *Damn it, Lily. Just deal with one thing at a time.* My mantra had always been to deal with stuff as it came. Worrying about it before time didn't make a difference, except to my stress levels. So I pushed problem two out of the way and made problem one my first priority, which made total sense.

Should I wait here for Daniel to come see what was going

on? Did I even have time before Tom woke up? Probably not. Instead, I'd have to wait for the distraction and put myself out in the open to get to Daniel. I was pretty sure Abby had understood me, but she was taking her sweet time organising a squirrel insurgence.

As much as I wanted to stab Daniel in the eye with my heel, it was a high-risk manoeuvre. It was less risky to go with my pot plant. He'd done such a good job on Tom, and he had another head-clobbering in him. I dropped my shoes and picked up the pot. "I think I'll call you Pete. Thanks for helping, Pete."

Squirrel chittering reached me, and a loud, angry meow.

That was my cue.

I hugged Pete to my chest, reluctant to step out into the open. My spine prickled. I wanted to shut my eyes and disappear. But that wasn't an option. *You can do this. No time to hesitate. Think of Beren and Liv.*

I swallowed, took a deep breath, and ran.

Liv, Daniel, and the celebrant were facing towards the forest, bent over, trying to shoo away the twelve or so squirrels who were attacking their lower legs. Thankfully, they were striking and running, striking and running. That way, no one could kick them. Crafty little squirrels. I wasn't too worried that they were attacking Liv—I was pretty sure they were just keeping her occupied so they could wreak more havoc on Daniel. I hoped their claws were getting through his pant legs.

Liv yelled, "Ow!"

The language Daniel used would've made a pirate proud.

Ah, good, they were getting through the pant legs.

I was halfway across the yard, breathing hard, legs pumping as fast as I could push them. This was the only time I would be happy about that colossal split in my dress.

Please don't see me. If they turned around now, I was toast.

I was almost there.

Then the stupid celebrant saw me. "Help!" Okay, so he only wanted me because there was a squirrel on his back, but his outburst made Daniel turn.

Crap.

Daniel's eyes widened, and he straightened and swore. So much swearing. He wasn't happy, which was the only amusing thing I could see in this situation.

I had no idea if he was drawing magic or not. This could all be about to end badly.

A brownish blur shot from the trees and bounded up his back before jamming itself on his head and reaching claws around to scratch the crap out of his face. Abby! Oh, God, what if he hurt her?

Now that he was distracted, I was safe for a few seconds. More squirrels poured out of the forest. Holy moly. There must be thirty or forty. They scampered every which way like out-of-control firecrackers, and I couldn't count them properly.

My squirrel army had arrived! A momentous occasion I'd waited months for. If only I had more time to savour my success.

Focus, Lily.

Daniel had managed to get a hand on Abby. No! I reached him, but I couldn't hit him in the head because Abby was there, and he'd grabbed her leg so she couldn't escape. Crap.

The squirrels were trying to help. Both his legs were covered in grey fluffballs of doom, and two had latched onto his stomach. Surely soon he'd regain his composure enough to magic them away.

There was only one thing to do.

I stood in front of the squirrelly mass of bad man, bent my

knees, and swung the pot down and back between them, then pushed my hips forward, and flung the pot up into his crotch.

Bullseye!

"Aaaaarghhhh!" He grunted. His hold on Abby disintegrated, and as he dropped forward to clutch his crotch, she jumped free. I changed my grip on the pot and smashed him in the back of the head.

He fell forward and face planted into the ground. Two out of two. My strike rate today was phenomenal. Now to get Liv away from here.

I grabbed her arm as she tried to swat a squirrel from her leg. "We have to get out of here. They've probably got rabies or something."

She looked at me, a mixture of shock and confusion on her face. "What's going on?"

"Abby, tell the squirrels they can stop now. And thank them profusely. We need to get out of here, so come with me." She meowed, and the squirrels scampered away. Abby leaped into my arms. "Good girl." She nuzzled my neck, and Liv gave me a curious look. I flicked my gaze to Daniel. Had his magical hold on Liv's mind loosened now he was unconscious? "Do you know who that is?" I asked, pointing at Daniel.

Her brow furrowed. "Oh my God. What's Beren doing on the ground? And what's all that blood?" She started to kneel next to him, but I grabbed her arm and kept her up.

I did a mental happy dance for Abby's deft claws. He deserved every scratch and bite he suffered. "It's not Beren, just someone who looks identical. You were kidnapped. Do you remember being in your house when he took you?"

She worried her lip. "I— I'm not sure."

"Do you remember how you got into that dress?"

She put a hand to her forehead and pressed. "Vaguely, but it seems like a dream."

"Hey!" Tom stood at the front of the house, but he was leaning heavily on the wall, and his voice wasn't very loud.

There was no more time to explain. "Do you trust me?"

"Yes, of course."

"I don't have my magic, and they're bad guys. We need to run. Right now."

She nodded, threw off her shoes, and joined me as we ran for the front of the house and past Tom. He tried to follow but stumbled and stopped, legs bent, hands bracing on his thighs. "Where are you going?"

"Out of here. You'd better help Daniel. He's in trouble!" That should get him off our backs. I didn't wait to see whether he took the bait or not. I ran faster, Liv just in front of me. We reached the driveway. Gravel stabbed into my soles, but the pain was a small price to pay for escape. Hopefully, Tom didn't have any healing skills to speak of. At least he was a slow thinker and hadn't stopped us.

Liv reached the road first. "Which way?"

I stopped next to her, swivelling my head back to check we hadn't been followed. So far, so good. I looked up and down the street. In the distance, down a slight hill, looked to be the start of a village, but it was still probably half a mile away. I pointed towards it. "That way. We need to keep running."

"Okay." God, I loved her when she wasn't under a spell. She trusted that I had her back. The original and best Olivia was back.

"Abby, keep a lookout over my shoulder. Let me know if Danial comes after us."

She meowed. I assumed, for my sanity, that she'd said yes.

We'd be faster if I didn't have to look over my shoulder every five seconds.

All I could say about sprinting down the road was thank God I'd kept up with my fitness when I came to the UK. As it was, my breath rasped painfully in my throat, my mouth was dry, and I felt like not enough oxygen was going in for the effort my body made. *Just keep going.*

"*Meow.*"

I risked a glance behind. "Crap. Daniel's after us."

We had a good four hundred feet on him. I didn't know how far magic could travel, but hopefully we were out of striking range. The rumble of a car came from his direction and crested the hill behind us. I waved at it with one arm. "Liv, wave too."

She half turned as she ran, her arm pumping up and down. The red car slowed to a halt. I ran around to the driver's side; a blonde woman about my age with a gorgeous face and big green eyes looked at me. "Are you okay?" Oh my God, she was Australian. I'd know that accent anywhere.

"Those men back there are after us. Can we please get in?"

She shifted her gaze to the rear-view mirror, then scrunched her face. Her eyes widened, and she swivelled her head back to me. "Yes. Get in!"

A sparking sizzle came from behind us. I turned my head to look. The footpath about thirty feet away exploded, concrete and dirt shooting into the air above it like a dirty fountain. The woman in the car let out a short scream. Liv and I looked at each other, wide-eyed, across the top of the car. Then I jumped into the back seat, and Liv hopped into the front passenger seat. I looked behind. They were only fifty feet away. "Drive! Drive!"

The woman slammed her foot down. I shot back into the

seat, and Abby mewled. "Sorry, kitty. I didn't mean to squeeze so hard." I loosened my hold on her enough so she could breathe. Probably also best to put my seat belt on if I was going to ask our new friend to drive like a demon was chasing us.

The woman's hands were shaking on the steering wheel. "W— What the hell of all hells was that?"

Without knowing whether she was a witch, I couldn't say much. "I don't know. Maybe they have explosives?"

"Right. Okay." She mumbled something else to herself.

Liv turned to her as we reached the village. "We're so sorry, but thank you so much for picking us up. Can you just drive us to the next village?"

"Oh. Ah, okay. That's where I'm going anyway, I think." She met my gaze in the rear-view mirror. She shook her head as if to shake off... something. "Is that an Aussie accent I detect?"

I smiled. "Yes. I'm from Sydney. What about you?"

She grinned, and her face relaxed. "Me too! I'm from Narrabeen. What about you?"

"Cronulla."

"Ha, cool. I'm Avery, by the way."

"I'm Lily, and this is my best friend Liv."

"Hi." Liv gave a small wave and an even smaller smile, like she hadn't yet worked out what had happened. If she'd basically just come out of a trance, it would be similar to waking up when your house is burning down, and you have to get the hell out of there. There's no time to take stock and get everything straight. Because Avery could be a non-witch, there was no way I could explain properly. Poor Liv would have to wait. The main thing was that we were safe. Except bloody Daniel and Tom were alive and free. If they ran, we'd have a hell of a time finding them. Crap. Today had to be a record for how many times I'd thought that word.

"Do you need to call someone?" Avery asked. "You can use my phone."

"Really? That's so nice of you. Thank you."

"It's in my bag, Liv. Just grab it out."

"Are you sure?" Liv asked, probably wary of going through someone else's personal belongings.

"Totes."

Liv bent and grabbed the bag from next to her feet, then pulled it onto her lap and rummaged through. "Passcode?"

"654321." Avery chuckled. "Yeah, it's stupid, I know, but I've never lost a phone, and I didn't want to make it too hard to remember."

Liv managed a chuckle. "I hear you." She punched the numbers in and handed me the phone. "You do it. I'm not sure what to say."

I dialled Will, hoping he wouldn't ignore the strange number. "Hello, Agent Blakesley speaking."

Relief filled me, squeezing tears from my eyes. My voice was shaky. "Will, it's Lily. I had to borrow a phone."

"Lily! Oh my God. Where are you? What happened?"

"I don't know where I am. Daniel's mate kidnapped me, and he took me to where Daniel had Liv. We've hopped into a kind lady's car, and she's taking us to a village. This is her phone."

"Okay, understood. What happened to your magic?"

"The guy, Tom, snapped a *bracelet* on me."

He swore. "Okay. Is Liv all right?"

"Yes. She's with me now. Hang on a sec." I looked at Avery. "What's the next town called, the one we're going to?"

"Manesbury."

I relayed the information. "Can you come get us ASAP?"

"Of course. Hang on a sec." His voice came through. He was asking Angelica about that town. After a moment, she said something I couldn't quite catch. "Lily, have the woman drop you at the post office. One of our retired agents lives a few houses down from there. He's in his nineties, so his magic isn't very strong anymore, but we can use his reception room. We'll see you there as soon as you get there."

"Okay, thank you." I hung up and handed the phone back. We made small talk for the ten minutes it took to reach the village.

Avery stopped in front of the post office, a two-storey free-standing stone building with a thatched roof and red front door. "Are you two sure you'll be okay?"

I nodded. "Yes. Thank you so much. You literally saved our lives. That guy and his mate kidnapped us and dressed us in these stupid dresses."

Avery gave Liv the once over. "It looks like something a stripper might wear to her wedding."

Liv looked down at herself, maybe noticing for the first time. "Oh, my. You can almost see my underwear."

Avery chuckled. "Almost, but not quite. Your modesty in that area has been preserved. Your cleavage, however, is another story."

Liv's cheeks darkened, and she placed a hand over her boobs, which were almost fully exposed. "Oh, God." Unfortunately, I had nothing to give her to cover up. At least the boys would be here any moment, but we didn't want Avery to see. She'd likely be confused as to how our friends got here so quickly—and we had no good answers.

"You can stay behind me, Liv. Come on." I hopped out and leaned in Avery's window. "Thank you so, so much. You really are a lifesaver. I owe you one. If you ever need a favour, just ring that number that's in your phone. That's my boyfriend, Will. He'll give you my number."

She smiled as Liv got out of the car. "Will do. Feel free to call me and let me know if the police catch those guys. I'm not sure if I should've moved here now. I just flew in from Oz yesterday."

"This was personal. You should be fine. But I'll let you know when we catch them... um, when they're caught, rather. Good luck, Avery. I hope your move turns out to be awesome."

"Me too." She turned and pulled a face at her back seat—okay, that was weird—then turned back to me, waved, and drove away slowly. The main street didn't look super long, so she probably didn't have too far to drive before she had to turn off and look for her new house. Maybe she was just tired and overwhelmed, especially after travelling all the way from Australia, then picking up two strange women who were dressed like they were trying to pick up at a nightclub but had no shoes on and were running away from kidnappers who may or may not have thrown explosives at them.

Just another day for Liv and me, really. But maybe not for Avery. Yeah, welcome to the UK, lady. May your life here be way smoother than mine. If she wasn't a witch fraternising with PIB agents, she should be fine.

Speaking of which, Will, James, Imani, and Angelica came out of a small laneway and hurried towards us. They weren't in uniform—because that would definitely stand out here. Will started jogging as soon as he saw us. He reached us first and swept me into his arms, squishing me tight. Abby, caught in the middle, meowed. He buried his face into my neck, and I could hear him sniff. "Are you smelling me? Also, you're suffocating Abbs."

"Sorry, cat, but you'll have to be patient. Yes, Lily, I was sniffing you. I just want to breathe you in for a moment. You have no idea how scary it was. There was a text message on my phone from Daniel, saying he'd taken you and I had Beren to thank for it. He sent it from Liv's phone but then switched it off so we couldn't track it."

Angelica asked Liv a couple of questions as to her health, and Imani had her arms around her.

I gave Will a last squeeze, then pulled away. "He's probably getting away right now. We can take you to the house, but we'll need a car. I'm not walking three miles."

Angelica regarded me. "What in the world are you two wearing, or not wearing, as the case may be?"

"Daniel dressed us for the wedding. He's not a fan of modesty, and the shoes he made us wear weren't good for running."

Her poker face crumbled. "Wedding?!"

"Don't worry; it didn't go ahead. Abby and our squirrel army made sure of that."

Liv smiled. "And Lily with her pot plant."

"Ah, yes, Pete proved to be a competent ally."

James shook his head. "You can tell us the full story later. Right now, we need to get back to that house. Imani's going to take Liv home, and you can show us where it is. Is that okay, Lily?"

"Totally." I handed Abby to Liv. "Take her with you. She's good for a few cuddles."

"Thanks." She gave me a half smile. Her eyes, though, had a haunted look. Likely, she was still trying to process things. And how would she feel when she saw Beren again? What if Daniel had ruined Beren for us forever? No! Beren was the original and a good person. Surely this one experience couldn't affect how we felt around him. I'd be willing to have a mind wipe if it came to that. The past few days were ones I'd happily live without.

"Wait here." Angelica walked back with Imani and Liv.

"Where's she going?"

"To get retired Agent Phillips's car."

"Oh, that's good."

James grabbed my hand and held it up. "This is the bracelet?"

"Yes. Think you could unlock it?" Goosebumps popped up along my arm. "It's getting a bit nippy. What time is it?" The sun had mostly gone, the last orangey-pink rays colouring the ground and the silver metal of my shackle.

"I'll try when we're in the car." He took off his long-sleeve T-shirt, revealing a short-sleeve T-shirt underneath. "Put this on."

"Thanks, bro. You're the best." I pulled the top on and instantly felt warmer. My ears pricked up. "Is that a VW Beetle I hear?" The loud puttering behind us couldn't be anything else…. At least, I didn't think it was a lawnmower. I giggled at an image of the four of us standing on a lawn-mower making our way up the hill.

Will stared at me, concern in his eyes. "Are you all right?"

"Yeah, why?"

"You're laughing for no apparent reason."

James smirked. "And?" I held my hand up, and he high-fived me.

Will rolled his eyes and opened the back Beetle door for me to slide in. "Okay, humour me. Tell me what's so funny." I explained about us and the mower. He pulled a "you have to be kidding me face." "That's not funny."

"You clearly have no sense of humour." I shrugged and

slid over so he could get in. James jumped into the front seat, and Angelica pulled away from the kerb.

James turned to look at me. "Show me the magic blocker." I gave him my hand. He put his hand over it and shut his eyes. The metal vibrated. "Give me a minute." As he worked on it, I kept an eye out for the driveway. After a couple of minutes, James grunted, and the bracelet heated enough to sting.

"Ouch!"

"Just a sec." Sweat beaded on his forehead. The click as the bracelet unlocked was barely audible over the noise of the car.

"Oh my God, you did it! Thank you!" He kept the manacle, and I rubbed my wrist. A blister was already forming on the delicate underside. I drew on my power, filling my blood with heat. "Ahhhh, that feels good." I cut it off and smiled. "Man, I hope Daniel is still there when we go back."

Will raised a brow. "You're not allowed to kill him unless you have no choice."

I pouted. "Aw, you're spoiling all my fun. Look at what he dressed me in, and he tried to ruin Beren's life! He's killed, kidnapped, and framed. Life in jail is too good for him."

"Lily…." Will's tone held a note of warning.

"Yeah, yeah, I know." I imitated Will's voice. "No killing Daniel."

"That's a good impersonation, dear."

"Why, thank you, Ma'am." I sat up straight as I stared out the window. There was the hole from the explosion. "The place is just up here on the right."

Angelica slowed the car, and soon, I told her where to turn. I put up my return to sender. "Is it far to the house?"

"No. A short walk."

"I'd rather we didn't announce our arrival so loudly." She

turned into the driveway and stopped. "This will do. We can walk from here." She turned the car off. "I don't expect they'll still be here, but just in case, Lily, you stay with me at the rear. James and Will can take the lead."

"Okay. Just so you know, living areas are downstairs, bedrooms up. The wedding was in the backyard, and Daniel and his mate Tom both had throwing knives. They were playing with them before the wedding."

Thunder rolled into Will's expression. "They better not have touched you with those… or anything else."

"No, they didn't. They were throwing them in the back-yard, and Liv hadn't… you know… with fake Beren."

Will's expression lost some of its tightness, but not enough. He was still livid. Something told me that I wasn't the one who needed reminding that no one was allowed to murder anyone, no matter how deserving they were.

Angelica gave a nod. "Let's go."

We all jumped out of the car and started along the drive-way. Will and James took their guns out. I had to admit, Will was the epitome of sexy, even without his suit on. He'd make a great James Bond, and he was all mine. I grinned. How lucky was I?

I could tell Angelica held her power because her aura glowed brighter than usual. I opened my portal, just in case. *Remember: no lightning. No killing.*

Not that I was in the mood for more danger, but I hoped they were there. I wanted this over and done with and Beren out of jail. And we were four against two. Easy-peasy, right?

The house came into view, but no one was in the front yard. As we sneaked closer to the house, James halted and held up his hand for us to stop. My hyperaware hearing picked up my pulse thudding fast. I stopped breathing and listened, hoping to hear what had made him stop.

Instead of an attack, James pulled his phone from his pocket. He made a bubble of total silence. Angelica stared at him, her poker face intact. We didn't have to wait long. Within a minute and half of answering the phone, he'd hung up and dropped the bubble. He didn't bother speaking in a quiet voice, and it was soon apparent why. "Emergency. There's an attack on Beren's parents' home."

"Those magical alarms I installed are obviously working, then. I'll make the doorway." She looked at me. "We'll let the boys go first, dear." Angelica made her doorway. The guys went through, and she turned to me. "On second thoughts, we probably won't need you right now. Go home, and I'll come get you when it's over so you can stay safe. Collecting evidence can wait till later."

"Okay. If you say so." Wow, getting let off was good, although I had been looking forward to hurting Daniel and Tom just a little bit.

"I do." She gave a nod, stepped through, and the doorway disappeared.

Maybe I should take that guy's car back? That would be the polite thing to do since everyone else had forgotten—admittedly, they'd had a good reason to rush off.

"Hey, bitch!" Magic crawled on my scalp a second before the ground beside me exploded, spearing me with dirt and gravel and throwing me a few feet away. I landed hard on my shoulder and side, grunting with the impact.

Crap. Daniel.

I turned my head to look at him. He stood near the front door, which was open, and he had a return to sender up. Argh!

We'd been had. I hadn't figured he'd be super smart, but Beren was, so it stood to reason his brother would be. Just because he was evil didn't mean he was stupid. Worse luck for us.

He took a few steps forward and stopped. "People who get in my way get what's coming to them."

I ignored the ache in my shoulder and leaped up, pretending I was fine. If he saw any weakness, he would exploit it. "Aw, you sad Liv left you at the altar? You're clearly the inferior brother. How does the rejection feel?" My arms were ready to fend off the next attack. If he started channelling magic again, I'd run, make it harder for him. In the meantime, I had to think of what to do to him.

Scalding anger hazed his eyes. He took another step towards me, and I smirked as if I had something planned. He stopped. I grinned. "Aw, scared of little old me? I'm just a woman. What could I possibly do?" He'd read Liv's mind, so he knew. The irritated expression on his face proved it.

But he managed to shake it off. "Die!" His magic fired up, and I ran towards him—I figured that the closer I was to him, the less he could blow stuff up because he'd get caught in it. It was a genius idea that I was quite proud of. I didn't know how I came up with this stuff sometimes. But thank God I did.

The explosion hit where I'd been standing. Gravel pebbled my back and bare shoulders, but it only stung. Stupid dress. "Is that all you've got? Always the loser. If only you were Beren, you wouldn't have to attack women to get their attention."

His face twisted in rage, and I stopped a few feet from him. "You women are all the same. Throw us away when you don't want us. Because of you lot, I had a shitty life, and my brother was treated like a prince. You're not taking it away from me now." His magic scraped my scalp, but I was quicker. I'd spied Pete's twin, Paul, sitting on the front porch. I translocated him to the edge of the porch roof, so he was more off than on. And because I'd bought myself some time being so close to Daniel —he couldn't blow me up, so he'd had to change tack—my ploy worked perfectly. Paul finally overbalanced and fell.

He smashed onto the top of Daniel's head. His eyes rolled up in their sockets before he collapsed in blood, dirt, and silence.

Oops. I hadn't killed him by accident, had I? I covered the remaining few feet to him and felt for a pulse. It was faint. I didn't have a phone, and he needed treatment. There was only one place to take him.

I made a doorway and dragged him through.

CHAPTER 10

I'd dragged Daniel through to the PIB reception room and buzzed. Thank God Gus answered. He took one look at Daniel and did a double take. Once I convinced him it wasn't Beren, he helped me drag him down to the cells. My plan was for Beren to heal him so we could then lock him up instead and show Chad.

We'd put Daniel on the bed, and Beren and I stared down at him while Gus watched from outside the locked cell. Daniel's breathing was shallow, but still there. Beren had both hands linked behind his head, and he was just shaking his head, whispering, "No way. No way. No way. How can this be?"

I folded my arms. I wanted to give him a hug, but he needed space to digest this. And if I'd thought seeing Bad Beren do evil things was disconcerting, seeing both of them in the same room was freakier. At least they were wearing different clothes—not like it would be in the movies so you couldn't tell them apart. One good thing was that when I looked at Beren, I knew who he was, and I didn't hate him or worry he wasn't him. I didn't expect him to do anything untoward, and he wasn't creepy.

The main door to the cell area opened, multiple footsteps echoing off the hard surfaces. James, Will, and Angelica reached the cell, and James unlocked it. "Gus told us what happened." He looked at the twins as everyone else filed in—it was getting crowded in here. Other than staring longer than was necessary, James hid his shock well. He focussed solely on Beren. "Are you okay with healing him?"

Beren jammed his lips closed, and his jaw muscles bulged. "How's Liv?"

"She's going to be fine," Angelica said. "She's safely with Imani."

"And my parents?"

"They weren't home at the time of the attack. There'll be some repairs to do, but that's it."

Beren stared down at Daniel again, his gaze hard, flinty, un-Beren-like. I shivered at how close Daniel had come to ruining all our lives. Beren was a forgiving person, a good guy, but maybe this was just too much.

"We need him, B." Will, always the voice of reason. "We want you out of here and him in. Knowing you-know-who, he won't believe our version of events if he dies. He'll at least make things difficult."

Beren shut his eyes for a few moments. He dropped his hands, and they slapped as they hit the sides of his legs. He opened his eyes. "I'll save him, but get me out of here as soon as I'm done."

James placed a hand on his shoulder. "Understood." James took a minute and whispered a few words. Like the last time James had done this, the ozone odour enveloped us, and the air pressure in the room changed momentarily. "You should be good to go, mate."

Beren knelt next to the bed. His forehead wrinkled. "Lily, you dropped a pot on his head. How did he get all these scratches? Is that a bite mark?"

I was careful of what I said because now wasn't the time to tell him about the almost-wedding. "So Liv and I could escape, I borrowed a squirrel army. Abby managed to come through the doorway with me when I was taken. She makes a good general." I smirked. "You should've seen them savage him. It was beautiful to watch. I'd highly recommend you get some at the PIB. I'm telling you, they'd be an asset, and you'd only have to pay them peanuts."

My lame joke pulled a small smile from Beren, and one shade of darkness lifted from his eyes. Unfortunately, there were many more to go before his gaze shone brightly again. "Thanks, Lily. Once again, you've outdone yourself."

I smiled. "My pleasure, B. I'd do it again in a second."

He turned back to the bed and put his hands on his brother's scalp. As he worked, Angelica asked, "What happened?" Speaking quietly so as not to disturb Beren, I told them.

Will smirked. "You dropped a pot plant called Paul on his head?"

I nodded. "Yep. The squirrels were good the first time, but I didn't want him hurting them, and he was pretty angry. At the wedding, he was more surprised than anything. Also, we have to take that car back. And what about Tom, his accomplice?"

Angelica waved. "I have someone taking care of it, dear. Don't worry. And as for Daniel's associate, he's been arrested and is currently undergoing questioning in an interview room."

I breathed out my relief. "Yay on the car, and thank goodness Tom won't be out there wandering around."

Will looked at me. "I think Tom got off lightly compared to his mate." He nodded towards the bed. "You're lucky you didn't kill him."

"Yeah, well, I was just trying to survive, and I didn't have much time to plan nice ways to capture him—he had a return to sender up. Besides, I could've dropped Paul from the second-storey roof, and I chose not to."

One side of his mouth curled up. "That's my girl. Showing restraint. I'm proud of you."

I looked at Beren. "I'm not sure how happy he is about it though. Maybe he would've preferred I'd gone with the second-storey option."

"He'll deal. This whole thing's been a shock for everyone, but we'll help him through." There was no doubt in Will's tone that we would all make sure Beren was whole again.

"You're all good people."

We stood around for twenty minutes as Beren pushed himself to the limit to put his brother's head back together. Shame he couldn't cure the psycho tendencies while he was in there.

I looked at Angelica. "He's probably read Liv's mind and knows my secrets. Can you do a mind wipe tomorrow?"

She nodded. "Yes, of course."

"Thanks."

Daniel groaned, and Beren took his hands off his brother's head and leaned back. He bowed his head, his voice muffled. "I'm done." James reached down, grabbed Beren under the arms, and helped him up. He handed him off to Will. "Take him back to Angelica's. I don't want him and Liv alone tonight. I'll sort out Chad." He cocked his head to the side.

"Come to think of it, it's late, and he's probably at home watching TV. He won't even realise Beren isn't in here if we don't tell him. We can come clean in the morning. In the meantime, I'll have one of our medics check on Daniel every hour." Daniel hadn't opened his eyes. He would be sleeping off the effects of the healing for quite a while. Beren had pulled out all the stops to heal him if the time he took was anything to go by.

Will looked back at me as he reached the open cell door with Beren. "Come on. Let's get him home."

"Sounds good to me."

When we'd all exited the cell and the door clanked shut, I couldn't help the satisfied smile that graced my face.

Today the good guys had won.

Today was a great day.

CHAPTER 11

We spent the evening eating dinner and laying out everything, then hearing Liv's account of what happened. Mum even congratulated me on a job well done. Maybe she was coming around to the idea that I wasn't helpless.

Unfortunately, and expectedly, Liv couldn't remember everything, and what she did tell us was hazy. She gave permission to Angelica to dig around a little bit, more for evidence gathering than anything. The only person Angelica relayed the information to was James. They would be putting the case against Daniel together, whether Chad liked it or not.

And Millicent had discovered where all that money for expensive house rentals and paying note-delivery people off had come from. Beren's bank account. As soon as Beren was arrested, Daniel had gotten access to his account with fake ID and some magic.

The next morning, James called Chad, and we all went in, including Liv and Beren. It was as if a plough churned up furrows in my belly. Would Chad lose it and fire everyone, then stick Beren back in jail? Surely he didn't have the power to go against the law? He did have a skill with twisting things to suit himself—he made the illogical logical so that it only made sense to him. Although, we might have the upper hand with that spell that bounced back to him. Unless whoever instructed him to cast it in the first place realised it was in his aura and removed it....

As we walked along the hallway towards the conference room, it was like a funeral procession. We were quiet, guarded —a processing procession. My play on words wasn't enough to make me smile. Bummer. Beren and Liv walked holding hands. Since they'd been reunited, they hadn't spent a moment apart, with the exception of going to the toilet... I was assuming, anyway.

Before we reached the door, Angelica, who was leading us, stopped and turned. "Gather around for a moment." We did as asked, and she made a bubble of silence. "We probably should've discussed this before, but with everything going on, I forgot to mention it." She raised a brow at me. "Yes, Lily, I'm sure you're amused that the great Ma'am wasn't 100 per cent organised." Who could blame me for smirking? It wasn't often I got the chance to enjoy a Ma'am mistake. She turned back to the group. "Anyway, as you know, the spell he tried to cast on Lily bounced back and hit him. We have an opportunity, via Lily, to ask him questions he'll have to answer—provided the spell is still intact. If it is, we need to tread lightly. There are things I'd like to know, but there are certain questions that may put us even more in the firing line from the directors. If we know secret business they want hidden, we potentially become an even bigger problem for them."

Will frowned. "And we'll be gone sooner rather than later."

She gave a nod. "Exactly." She gave everyone a firm look. "Also, we don't want them to know we suspect anything. Leave all the sensitive questions up to me." She smiled. "Are we clear?"

"Crystal," we all replied. I grinned. That was some cool synchronicity. Talk about teamwork.

Angelica tipped her chin and walked the last fifteen feet to the conference room. She opened the door and led us in.

Showtime.

I kind of wished I had my bee costume on since it had gotten such a good reaction last time. Maybe I'd chuck in a couple of buzzing noises when he least expected it.

Chad was sitting in his usual spot at the head of the table. He eyed us suspiciously as we entered, and when he saw Beren, his mouth fell open. When he recovered the power of movement, he shot to his feet and pointed at him. "What the heck are you doing here?" He turned to James and yelled, "Get him back in the cells! That's an order!"

"His identical twin brother, Daniel, is the murderer, not Beren. He also kidnapped Olivia and Lily."

Everyone was still standing, and we made a circle around him. It wasn't a conscious thing, and it made me think of wolves. James's magic prickled my scalp, and a video screen appeared on the wall. "Look. Here's a live feed from the cells."

The image showed Daniel sitting on his bed, back resting against the wall, arms folded. He had dark circles under his eyes from the healing. His frown and pout left no question as to how he was feeling—angry and resentful. Chad walked up to the screen as if he couldn't believe his own eyes. He turned to us and put his hands on his hips. "You expect me to believe this?" He waved his arm to indicate the screen behind him. "I didn't feel your magic, but this has to be a trick."

James had to remain professional, but I did not. I rolled my eyes. "Go and see for yourself. Make a beeline for the cells. Bzzzzzzz." I grinned. Imani covered her mouth and turned her laugh into a cough.

He stared at me. He grinned as if having outsmarted us. "I will." He made a doorway and stepped through.

That was unexpected. "How can he make a doorway to there? There's no landing spot, and it's secure."

Angelica looked at me. "There's a special landing spot calibrated for whoever happens to be running operations. It's in a room on the same floor as the cells, a couple of doors away from the observation room. I tended not to make a doorway there in front of others. The less everyone knows, the better. I expect you to keep it to yourselves."

I imagined James knew, since he'd taken her role before Chadiot had come. James managed to keep it quiet, but of course Chad was, well, an idiot. He soon appeared in the cells, standing outside. He said something we couldn't hear—this was a video feed only. Daniel looked at him, then said something back. Their conversation lasted five minutes before Chad left. He had to take the long way back to us. Eventually he walked through the door.

"It appears as though you're right—that is his twin. But he says he didn't do anything."

Angelica closed her eyes and slapped her forehead. Wow, there was even only so much she could take. Although, it was her nephew at the centre of this disaster. Chad gave her a dirty look. She shrugged. "The mosquitoes are bad this time of year."

"Bzzzzzzzz." Okay, so I couldn't resist. Bee noises became mosquito noises so easily. Chad turned his glare on me. I smiled innocently.

"Prove that Beren is innocent." He folded his arms.

"We have two witnesses right here." Angelica gestured towards Liv and me. "Lily was the one who brought Daniel in after he tried to blow her up, and Beren healed him because Lily had to use forceful measures. It will all be on last night's security video, if you care to watch it."

"Videos can be tampered with."

Angelica's face was pokered up, but her eyes were hard and cold. Things were about to get serious. My brother stepped in between her and Chad. James shook his head. "If you had the knowledge you should have being the head of PIB operations, you'd know that we spell our videos to make them tamper-proof." Whoa! Way to go, brother of mine. He was risking a lot by insulting Chad, but maybe he was beyond caring now. Too much was at stake.

"I'm willing to be placed under a truth spell," Liv said. "That man in the cell kidnapped me, put a coercion spell on me, and almost married me against my will. If you let him out, I'll go the newspapers and out the lot of you."

I blinked. That was a Liv I'd never seen before. I knew she wouldn't do that, but Chad didn't, and his face paled. Finally, he was beginning to pay attention. "Y— You can't do that! You've promised under magical oath."

"Oh, yes I can—I'm willing to suffer the consequences because this is important. And when the directors see I'm willing to testify under a truth spell, you won't have a leg to stand on. Look at the evidence."

"What evidence? The word of you and your friends?"

Angelica nudged James out of the way. "I've dispatched a crew to the house they were holding Olivia in. They're collecting evidence, and last night I took a statement from Olivia. Lily is going to give her statement later today. There is also another human witness we can call on who picked up the ladies when they ran from that house of horrors. All that time, Agent Beren DuPree was locked up downstairs." She stepped forward so she was toe to toe with him, her nose inches from his. "I won't back down on this. If you want a fight, bring it. I'm ready." The look she gave him could've destroyed someone ten times braver than him.

He ringed a finger around the inside of his collar, then loosened his tie, and I was pretty sure that was sweat beading on his forehead. He cleared his throat. "Fine. I'll look at the evidence, but I'll have to write up a special report since this involves one of our agents."

"You do what you have to, but if you let that man out of jail anytime soon, you'll regret it, director friends or no director friends." *Yes!* Angelica hadn't moved from her spot breathing in his face. It was satisfying watching her finally stand up to him. Either she'd come to the end of her tether, or she had a plan to go against the directors and was almost ready to make her move.

Then Chad did something surprising because I didn't think he had it in him. He lifted his chin. "You're covering something up for your nephew. I know you are. And once I've gone through the evidence, if I find anything untoward, you won't just be fired, all of you will be going to jail." Would he tamper with evidence, plant some? I met Will's angry gaze. Crap.

Angelica's poker face remained, but the icy calm radiating from her was jarring. She looked at me. My eyes widened, and I looked behind me. What did she want me for? "Lily, I've changed my mind. I want you to ask Chad some very important questions." My fearful look of why me was loud and clear. "Because you're the only one who can."

And then I got it. Chad's spell had bounced off me. I was the one he had to tell the truth to. The questions I was about to ask were dangerous, but who was I to argue with Angelica?

"Chad, why are the directors out to get us?"

His breath hitched, and his face turned white again. As a ghost. He pressed his lips together, but he was fighting the inevitable. "They're scared you'll find out the truth."

Everyone held their breaths and stared at Chad, waiting for the bomb to drop.

"And what truth is that?"

"Directors Brosnan and Craig are being paid off by a criminal syndicate to disband the PIB. We'll be shut down within three months, and I'll be safely back in the US with my bonus." He slapped his hand over his mouth and stamped his foot. I chuckled. Bad luck, Chadiot. You didn't just spill the beans; you spilled the whole enchilada.

Unfortunately, this wasn't a regular bomb. It was atomic. Angelica had the wherewithal to not look shocked, but Imani and Beren could both catch flies with their open mouths. I cleared my throat. "How much is your bonus?"

"Two million pounds."

"And what were the directors going to do if Angelica, or any of us, found out?"

This time Chad smiled. Dread ran a sharp nail down my spine. He might not have liked that we'd pulled the truth out of him, but he was enjoying this last bit too much for it to be anything good. "You just signed your own death warrants. Maybe it will be an assassin in the night. Maybe it will be a job gone wrong. It will be something no one can prove."

My stomach fell to the floor. Chadiot's bomb blew Angelica's poker face to smithereens. Will ground his teeth together —the noise turned my stomach. Beren and James stepped closer to Chad. I had no idea what they were going to do to him, if anything, but maybe it was just a gut reaction to the threat. Liv looked like she might throw up, and Imani grabbed her hand while shooting death stares at Chadiot.

I looked at Angelica and raised one eyebrow, an idea forming. "Well, we can't let them know that we know, right?"

She gave me a curious look, but then she smiled. "No, dear, we can't."

I drew my magic and cast a freeze spell on Chad. Will sucked in a breath. "Lily! What are you doing?"

Angelica's magic prickled my scalp, and Chad's hands came together in front of him. PIB handcuffs appeared on his wrists. Angelica turned towards the middle of the room and made a doorway, then turned back and looked at Will. "Will, dear, would you and James mind bringing Chad through my doorway? I'm afraid we have a lot of work to do, and we don't need him getting in the way."

James shook his head, his face bemused. Will opened his mouth to say something, closed it, opened it, closed it, opened it. He came to a decision eventually. "Okay, then."

James and Will picked Chad up and carried him through Angelica's doorway. Angelica waved at the rest of us. "Dinner, my place tonight at seven. Don't be late." She gave us a small smile and a wave, then stepped through and disappeared.

Imani scratched her head and looked at me. "Did we just kidnap the head of the PIB?"

I smiled. "Yep. I'm pretty sure that's what just happened."

"Now what do we do?" Liv asked.

I shrugged. "Beren's nemesis is in jail, and Angelica's is out of action. I'm pretty sure there's only one thing we can do."

Beren tilted his head to the side. "And that would be?"

"Why, celebrate, of course." I grinned and pretended that

I wasn't scared. We'd just done the most dangerous thing yet. We'd declared war on the directors of the PIB, only they didn't know it yet. When they eventually found out, we'd be in even more strife than we ever had been with RP.

Oh crap.

What the hell had we just done?

If you've enjoyed this book, you might enjoy my new cosy mystery series, Haunting Avery Winters. Book 1—A Killer Welcome—is out September 2021.

Avery Winters was overjoyed to be brought back to life... unfortunately, the dead were waiting for her.

Aussie journalist Avery Winters was content—she had a caring boyfriend, great job, and supportive... okay, so her parents weren't actually supportive, but she'd accepted she could never be the son they'd wanted seeing as how she was born a girl. Avoiding them seemed to work well, and, she reasoned, no one's life was perfect.

And that was fine, except whilst covering a news story in a storm, Avery's cosy life disappeared in a flash. Lightning struck, stopping her heart and blowing her favourite black boots to smithereens. It was pure luck that an off-duty nurse was walking nearby.

When Avery came to in the ambulance en route to hospital, she'd thought the worst was over. She was wrong.

Her lightning-induced hallucinations—there was no way they were ghosts—were impossible to hide. Her boyfriend soon left, and her boss suggested she take extended leave. Unable to cover her rent, she moved back in with her parents. And that's when the fun really began. Unable to cope with their insistence she was crazy, and desperate for an escape, she responded to a journalist-wanted ad… in the UK, because getting mega far away from her parents could only be a good thing.

Armed with a new fear of storms, companions others couldn't see, and the hope that leaving the stress behind would improve her mental state, she boarded a plane for London. What she didn't count on was not being able to leave her ghosts behind… literally. Oh, and that the quaint English village she'd be living in had more skeletons in its closet than the Natural History Museum.

When she stumbles upon a dead body in her rented apartment on her first day, she's tempted to get back on the plane. But whilst it's not a good omen, returning to her parents would be worse, so she decides to stay. Only, she's not sure if it's the best decision she's ever made, or the worst.

She's about to find out.

If you're after book 17 in the PIB series, it's coming July 2021.

ALSO BY DIONNE LISTER

The Circle of Talia

(YA Epic Fantasy)

Shadows of the Realm

A Time of Darkness

Realm of Blood and Fire

The Rose of Nerine

(Epic Fantasy)

Tempering the Rose

ABOUT THE AUTHOR

USA Today bestselling author, Dionne Lister is a Sydneysider with a degree in creative writing, two Siamese cats, and is a member of the Science Fiction and Fantasy Writers of America. Daydreaming has always been her passion, so writing was a natural progression from staring out the window in primary school, and being an author was a dream she held since childhood.

Unfortunately, writing was only a hobby while Dionne worked as a property valuer in Sydney, until her mid-thirties when she returned to study and completed her creative writing degree. Since then, she has indulged her passion for writing while raising two children with her husband. Her books have attracted praise from Apple iBooks and have reached #1 on Amazon and iBooks charts worldwide, frequently occupying top 100 lists in fantasy and mystery.